MONSTERIOUS

THE BEAST
OF SKULL ROCK

MONSTERIOUS
THE BEAST
OF SKULL ROCK

MATT MCMANN

putnam

G. P. Putnam's Sons

G. P. PUTNAM'S SONS
An imprint of Penguin Random House LLC, New York

First published in the United States of America by G. P. Putnam's Sons,
an imprint of Penguin Random House LLC, 2024

Copyright © 2024 by Matt McMann

Visit us online at PenguinRandomHouse.com.

Library of Congress Cataloging-in-Publication Data
Names: McMann, Matt, author.
Title: The beast of Skull Rock / Matt McMann.
Description: New York: G. P. Putnam's Sons, 2024. | Series: Monsterious; [4] |
Summary: While visiting their grandfather in a small New England town,
twelve-year-old twins Jade and Simon investigate a series of mysterious creature attacks.
Identifiers: LCCN 2023016106 (print) | LCCN 2023016107 (ebook) |
ISBN 9780593530788 (hardcover) | ISBN 9780593530801 (trade paperback) |
ISBN 9780593530795 (epub) | Subjects: CYAC: Twins—Fiction. | Siblings—Fiction. |
Monsters—Fiction. | Cities and towns—Fiction. | Mystery and detective stories. |
LCGFT: Detective and mystery fiction. | Novels.
Classification: LCC PZ7.1.M4636 Be 2024 (print) |
LCC PZ7.1.M4636 (ebook) | DDC [Fic]—dc23
LC record available at https://lccn.loc.gov/2023016106
LC ebook record available at https://lccn.loc.gov/2023016107

ISBN 9780593530788 (hardcover)

ISBN 9780593530801 (paperback)

1st Printing

Printed in the United States of America

LSCC

Design by Nicole Rheingans
Text set in Maxime Pro

Skull image courtesy of Shutterstock

To Mom & Dad, for believing I could touch the stars

CHAPTER 1

THE BEAST stepped from the narrow alley and paused in a patch of fading moonlight. Triangular ears twitched at a distant sound, far beyond the range of human hearing. Raising its muzzle, it sniffed the ocean breeze. Mingled with the salt water and restaurant scraps was another scent, one that brought a rumbling growl from the monster's broad chest.

It broke into a trot, slipping through the shadows like a ghost. Loping down another alley, the beast leaped and sank its claws into the wood siding on the back of a rambling two-story structure. It scaled the wall like a spider and dropped onto the flat roof. Padding soundlessly to the front of the building, the monster peered into the street below, keen eyes piercing the darkness.

A young girl with a canvas bag slung over her shoulder rode a bike through pools of light cast by old-fashioned streetlamps. Pulling out a folded newspaper, she tossed it against one of the many doors that lined the wooden boardwalk. As she approached the building that concealed her watcher, the monster tensed, muscles quivering as it prepared to pounce.

The light shifted as the ebony night gave way to an orange-and-purple glow. The beast's eyes snapped up and locked on the ocean's distant horizon. Its black lips curled into a snarl. With surprising lightness for its massive frame, the monster darted across the roof and over the side of the building. Noiselessly, it raised a window with its claws and slipped inside.

With a wide yawn, the girl continued tossing her papers as she biked into the rising sun.

CHAPTER 2

"I CAN'T wait to see the museum again!" Simon said, looking up from his book, *Escape from Grimstone Manor.* "And Grandpa."

His mother, Isabelle, glanced in the rearview mirror with a smile. "He and Mom love it when you two visit."

"I can't believe Grandma won't be there," Jade said as she gazed out the window at the passing trees. With her ivory skin and long dark hair, she was a twelve-year-old miniature of Isabelle.

"I'm really sorry, honey," Isabelle said. "When Aunt Geneviève got sick so suddenly, Grandma needed to go back to France to help out."

"It won't be the same," Jade said. "Who's going to do magic with me?"

"You can practice your tricks on me," Simon said. Unlike his twin sister, he'd inherited his father's darker complexion and wore his black hair short.

Jade smirked. "Well, you are easy to fool."

"I take back my offer," Simon said.

"You'll be busy enough without practicing magic tricks," Isabelle said. "Grandpa can't run the museum alone during tourist season, even if he thinks he can. And they can't afford to hire anyone right now." When her father called a few days ago with news of her mother's departure, he'd tried to convince her to reschedule the twins' visit. She'd insisted—not only did he need the help, she needed him to watch the twins during her upcoming anniversary trip to Greece.

"Don't worry, Mom, we've got this," said Simon. "The museum is awesome! I can't wait to see what creepy new displays Grandpa has put up."

"Almost there," Jade said as they passed a sign that read WELCOME TO SKULL ROCK, MAINE, POPULATION 7,432.

They entered a quaint downtown. Oceanside Lane was lined with charming historic buildings painted in bright colors. Well-maintained flower beds bordered the sidewalks between old-fashioned streetlamps. Art galleries, restaurants, antiques shops, coffeehouses, and clothing stores lined the redbrick street. The boardwalks were crowded with people window-shopping or sitting on sun-drenched benches eating ice cream. A grassy park with a white gazebo offered beautiful views of the nearby ocean. Rising above it all stood the town's name-sake, a large rocky cliff roughly shaped like a skull.

"There it is!" Simon exclaimed, pointing to a shop.

Isabelle parked in front of a sprawling two-story building. Above the front door hung a sign in swirling script—*Le Fantastique: A Cabinet of Curiosities Museum*. In the doorway stood a tall older man with wispy white hair and glasses that hung from a silver chain around his neck. The smile that creased his ivory skin couldn't banish a weary, anxious expression that clung to him like a stubborn vine.

"Grandpa!" the twins shouted as they threw open their doors. They wrapped Henri in a tight hug as the man chuckled.

"Do you have any new displays?" Simon asked excitedly.

"I guess you'll have to search the museum to find out," Henri said, a twinkle returning briefly to his eyes. Simon and Henri shared a love of unusual objects from around the world.

"Get your bags first," Isabelle said, opening the car's trunk. She walked over and hugged her father while the kids grabbed their bags and ran inside the museum.

"I call first pick of the beds," Jade said. She moved a PRIVATE—NO ADMITTANCE sign from the bottom of the stairwell and headed up the creaking steps to the second floor. At the top, she noticed the old wooden door to her grandparents' apartment had been replaced by a metal security one. Four parallel scratches marred the fresh gray paint. Jade paused, puzzling over the unusual marks. With a shrug, she continued to the guest room.

Ignoring his sister, Simon dumped his bags by the door and moved quickly through the gift shop into the museum. He paused and took in the huge room with a delighted smile.

The dimly lit space was filled with an amazing variety of strange, spooky artifacts. A two-headed taxidermy grizzly with twin gaping jaws stood menacingly on its hind legs. An eighteen-foot Nile crocodile hung suspended from the high ceiling. In a glass display case, a variety of stone knives were arranged on red velvet. On a long shelf sat an array of animal skulls, each in a miniature spotlight. The long, spiraling tusk of a narwhal lay on a table near glass jars filled with small creatures suspended in clear liquid. A cabinet contained a collection of jagged crystals with green, purple, and blue shards. Wooden chests and tall ornate vases decorated with paintings of monstrous creatures lined the aisles. Archways led to other tantalizing rooms, bursting with fascinating objects.

Simon stepped forward to explore as the front

door opened. "Not yet," his mother called. "You'll have all summer to do that. Put your things in your room, and we'll grab lunch before I have to leave."

Sighing, he took a last lingering look and turned away.

Unbeknownst to Simon, something in the museum looked back.

CHAPTER 3

"NOW PRESS that button," Henri said.

The drawer of the antique cash register popped open with a ping. Henri spent the afternoon teaching the twins how to sell admission tickets and souvenirs, dust the displays, sweep the floors, and stock the gift shop.

When the museum closed at five p.m., Henri took them down the street to Café Eiffel for crepes. The twins loved the thin pancakes stuffed with cheese, spinach, and prosciutto. Simon's dessert crepe was filled with chocolate hazelnut butter, while Jade's was loaded with strawberries and whipped cream.

Feeling pleasantly full, they wandered through the crowd along Oceanside Lane, enjoying the balmy summer evening. Henri led them to a storefront across the road from the museum. Hanging over the boardwalk was a wooden sign carved in the shape of a bird that read THE RAVEN: A BOOKSHOP.

"I want to introduce you to an old friend of mine," Henri said. "He moved here from France and opened this shop right after your visit last summer."

A bell jangled softly as they opened the door and stepped inside. The shop was small but cozy, with a high ceiling and polished woodwork that glowed in the lamplight. Tall shelves lined the walls and formed narrow corridors like the alleyways of a miniature city. They overflowed with beautifully bound books featuring engraved titles and gilded pages. The comfortable scent of leather and old paper hung in the air.

A man appeared at a wooden counter. The gray streaks in his short curly hair contrasted with his dark brown skin. He peered at them over gold-rimmed glasses that perched on the end of his nose. On the counter stood a large raven who flapped his wings and cawed loudly, staring at the visitors with an unblinking eye.

"Oh, la vache!" the man said in a French accent. "Jade, you look just like your mother. And, Simon, I am always glad to welcome a fellow book lover to my humble shop."

"Kids, this is Jacques," Henri said.

"Hey, Jacques," Simon said, surprised by the man's greeting. Jade gave an awkward wave.

"I apologize for being so familiar," Jacques said.

"I heard you were coming, and your grandfather talks of you so often, I feel like I know you already." The raven cawed again, and Jacques frowned at the bird. "Patience is a virtue. Edgar, this is Jade and Simon. Kids, this is Edgar."

The raven bobbed his head, then fluffed his feathers and began preening himself.

Jacques gave a wry grin. "Edgar thinks *he* runs this place. He is stubborn, like your grandfather. Did Henri tell you we knew each other back in France? He was as stubborn then as he is now. Like insisting on giving his museum a French name, 'Le Fantastique.' You are in a new country, I told him. Just call it 'The Fantastic.' Did I name my shop 'Le Corbeau'? No—'The Raven,' so people here can understand. But did he listen?"

"Why don't you two go look around?" Henri said with a chuckle. "Jacques and I have boring business things to discuss."

"Speak for yourself," Jacques said. "My books are never boring." He turned to the twins, his expression grave. "These books are valuable and très important to me. Can I trust you to handle them with respect?" When Jade and Simon nodded emphatically, he said, "Good. I would hate for Edgar to peck your eyes out."

Simon's face paled while Jade's eyes widened. She quickly narrowed them to give the bird a smaller target.

"Don't mind Jacques," Henri said to the twins. "His squawk is worse than his peck. Off you go."

The twins split up and wandered the aisles. Simon trailed his fingers gently over the spines of books as he walked. Finding *The Panther Man of Skull Rock and Other Legends*, he sank into a chair and began to read.

As Jade approached the back of the shop, Edgar landed on a nearby bookcase. She eyed the raven warily. "I'm not doing anything," she muttered, squinting protectively. When she began moving away, Edgar cawed. "What?" Jade asked. She took a second step, which drew another outcry from the bird.

With her brow wrinkled in confusion, Jade took a tentative step back toward Edgar. The raven stared at her. She walked until she was directly beneath him. As she gazed up at the bird, a thick blue book caught her eye. *The History of Magic* by Eliphas Levi was stamped on the spine in gold letters.

As she pulled the heavy book from the shelf, Edgar flew off. The grin that lit Jade's face at her discovery dimmed—she wished she could show this to her grandma Sophie. Their shared passion for magic had formed a special bond between them.

Replacing the book with a sigh, Jade strolled the aisles between the towering shelves, enjoying the comforting creak of the old wooden floorboards.

On hearing a sharp "psst!" she looked up and saw Simon motioning for her to join him near the front of the store.

"Do you need help with a big word?" Jade asked as she approached.

"Ha ha, I read better than you do," Simon whispered. "Listen."

The low murmur of conversation floated through the nearby shelves.

". . . probably local kids messing around," Henri said.

"I am not so sure," Jacques said. "*Two* shops on Oceanside broken into last week? Displays overturned, random things missing. Something is definitely going on, and I am not the only shop owner getting nervous. And what about the sightings?"

"You mean the Panther Man?" Henri scoffed. "Those are just rumors."

"Sometimes rumors are enough," Jacques replied.

"Enough to scare away the tourists you and I depend on to stay in business."

After an uncomfortable silence, Henri said, "But . . . the stories are ridiculous."

Jacques sighed. "I do not believe in this Panther Man any more than you do, but if word gets out . . ." He paused meaningfully.

"The mayor talked to Ingrid at the paper," Henri said. "She's going to keep a lid on this. Our summer business won't be ruined by *monster* sightings."

CHAPTER 4

"BUT WHAT if the sightings are real?" Simon insisted, pulling on his pajama shirt. He sat on his bed facing Jade in the guest room they shared in Henri's apartment above the museum. Not wanting to admit they were eavesdropping, neither twin had asked their grandpa about what they'd heard.

Jade flipped around on her bed to look at Simon. "You actually think there's a *monster* running around Skull Rock? You've been reading too many horror books."

"I've been reading the *right* horror books. There

have been Panther Man reports in this area for decades."

Jade sighed. "Okay, I'll bite. Who's Panther Man?"

"A tall, upright monster that's part human and part panther. He silently stalks his prey like a big black cat and drops down on them from above. He's rumored to live in the cave that forms the mouth of Skull Rock."

"That weird-looking rock formation above the town? How do you know all this?"

"There was a book about it in Jacques's shop. Plus I've heard about Panther Man on cryptozoology podcasts and in YouTube videos."

"Crypto-what?"

"Cryptozoology. The study of creatures not yet proven by science. You know, Bigfoot, the Loch Ness monster, Yeti, that kind of thing."

Jade rolled her eyes. "This town is about the last place I'd expect to find a monster."

"But that's just it!" Simon said. "Monsters show up in unexpected places. That's partly why they're scary."

"It's not monsters that scare me, unless they're, like, giant forest spiders or something," Jade said, her expression clouding. "But what if Jacques is right about the rumors driving away tourists? Grandpa wouldn't have to close the museum, would he?"

Simon paled. "He can't close the museum! It's the coolest place ever!"

"He might have to if he can't pay the bills." Jade rolled onto her back and stared moodily at the ceiling beams.

"Do you think that's why he seems kind of anxious?" Simon asked.

"He's definitely not himself," Jade said. "I wish we could help."

"We're giving him free labor," Simon said. "That's got to count for something."

"I guess." Jade's forehead furrowed as she re-membered the burglaries. "You don't think anyone will break into the museum, do you?"

Simon yawned. "Grandpa made a big deal at dinner about us not going downstairs at night be-cause of the security alarm, remember? Besides, if anyone comes, I'll protect you."

"Right," Jade said as she turned out the light. "I'll be the one protecting *you*."

Simon sat straight up in bed, eyes wide. A noise had woken him from a sound sleep. He checked his phone—12:04 a.m.—and listened intently.

A scraping sound came from the floor below, like a heavy object being shifted. Straining his ears, Simon thought he heard light footfalls.

Sweeping back the covers, he moved quickly

across the room. "Jade!" he whispered, shaking her shoulder. "Jade, wake up!"

She looked blearily at him and mumbled, "What the . . . Simon, get off my bed!"

"Shhh! I think there's someone in the museum."

A low growl rumbled up from below.

The twins stared at each other for a long moment, not daring to breathe. Then they jumped up and scrambled out the door. Moonlight poured through the kitchen window, illuminating the small apartment. They crossed the living room and entered Henri's bedroom without knocking.

"Grandpa!" Jade said as they ran over to the bed. "There's someone in the museum!"

"What?" Henri said groggily as he turned on his bedside lamp. "What are you talking about?"

"We heard noises!" Simon said. "Someone moving around. And a growl!"

Henri blinked rapidly and sighed. "This old building makes all kinds of noises. It creaks and groans as it settles. And there's the wind, water in the pipes, that kind of thing. Nothing to worry about."

The twins stared at him in surprise. "But the *growling*," Simon insisted.

"An easy mistake to make," Henri said. "But remember, I don't ever want you going down to the museum at night. You'd set off the security alarm. Now, why don't you go back to bed?" He fluffed his pillow and looked meaningfully at the door.

After sharing an uncertain glance, the twins said good night to Henri and walked slowly back to their room.

"Are you buying that?" Jade asked when they'd closed their bedroom door.

"I'm not sure what to think," Simon admitted, looking uncomfortable. "But why would Grandpa lie to us?"

CHAPTER 5

"WHAT WOULD you like to do on your day off?" Henri asked over breakfast the next morning. It being a Monday, the museum was closed.

"Jade and I want to go hiking," Simon said promptly.

She looked at her twin in surprise. "We do?"

"Yeah, we talked about it last night, remember?" Simon said, kicking her leg under the table.

She scowled at him before managing a weak smile. "Oh, yeah. You know I *love* hiking."

"Where are you thinking of going?" Henri asked. "Maybe I could come."

"We want to do the Cliffside Trail," Simon said. "It starts at the end of Oceanside Lane and goes all the way up to Skull Rock. My hiking app says the trail *is* rated difficult, though." Simon paused and gave Henri a questioning look.

"Difficult, huh?" Henri said. "That sounds a little adventurous for my old bones. Are you sure it's safe for you to go alone?"

"Oh, yeah," Simon said. "We hike by ourselves all the time back home, right, Jade?"

She plastered a grin on her face. "Yep."

After a moment, Henri nodded. "Skull Rock is close to town, so you should have cell service in case of an emergency. Don't be gone too long. Home for lunch, okay?"

"No problem," Simon said. "Thanks, Grandpa."

Once they were back in their bedroom with the door closed, Jade said, "You know I hate hiking. What's up?"

Simon held up his hands apologetically. "Sorry about that, but Grandpa gave me the opening, so I had to take it. Thanks for going along with it."

"Sure. But what am I going along with exactly?"

Simon grinned. "A monster hunt."

———

"I can't believe I let you talk me into this," Jade said an hour later, rubbing scrapes on her arm left by thorns. The narrow trail wound through towering pines and thick brush along the cliff edge.

"Come on, it's an adventure," Simon said. "We're trekking through a remote wilderness in search of a mythical beast that's terrorizing the town. Besides, it's better than wandering the tourist shops."

"But not better than going to the beach," Jade replied, panting as she waved away a mosquito. "And Panther Man? Really?"

"Why not? There are lots of creatures people thought didn't exist until they were proven by science."

"Name one."

"The coelacanth. It's a big lobe-finned fish that was supposed to be extinct for millions of years until one was caught off the coast of South Africa in the 1930s."

Jade gave him a wry smile. "You weren't supposed to have an answer for that. It was going to be my excuse for going back."

"Unwise were you, my monster knowledge to doubt," Simon said in a horrible Yoda impression.

The steep trail leveled off to a large rocky overlook. Jade caught her breath. Below them, the town of Skull Rock was laid out like a Christmas village.

A Christmas village in the middle of summer, but still. Miniature-looking cars drove slowly between the shops on Oceanside Lane. Beyond a long ribbon of beach, the endless ocean stretched to the far horizon. With a mournful cry, a seagull swept by the cliff at their feet.

"Not bad, huh?" Simon said.

Jade nodded, not taking her eyes from the scene.

Soon they turned and studied the cliff face behind them. The indents that formed the eyes and nose of Skull Rock were too close to distinguish, but the large cave that made the mouth yawned before them. They moved closer and peered into the gloom. The slanting rays of the midmorning sun illuminated the entrance of the cave, but beyond that was inky black.

Simon took a flashlight from his backpack. "You ready?"

As much as she'd made fun of Panther Man, the

thought of exploring the cavern made Jade uneasy. "Aren't there, like, bats in caves?"

"Yeah, but it's daytime, so they should be sleeping. Besides, they're tiny. Except for the golden-crowned flying fox. Their wingspan is almost six feet."

"You are not helping."

Simon grinned and stepped into the darkness. Jade reluctantly followed, staying close to her brother and the flashlight. As they picked their way over the rocky floor, Simon's light revealed rough stone walls streaked with rust-colored iron oxide. The floor was speckled with elongated brown pellets.

"What's all this stuff on the floor?" Jade asked.

"Guano," Simon replied. Seeing the confused look on her face, he added, "Bat poop."

"Ewww," Jade replied, scrunching her nose in disgust.

Simon pointed his flashlight at the high domed

ceiling, revealing a rippling mass of fur and leathery wings. Several pairs of beady red eyes peered down at them. Jade shuddered.

"So what's this Panther Man supposed to look like, anyway?" she asked as they moved deeper into the cave.

"He walks on two legs like a human, but has the head of a panther. Tall and muscular with sharp claws and glossy black fur."

"Does he have a tail?"

"People argue about that one."

They moved carefully, trying to avoid the guano. Soon the ceiling sloped downward and the sides converged to form a large tunnel. The twins walked around a bend, and the light from the now-distant opening disappeared.

Jade stopped. Even in the cool cave, her palms grew clammy and she felt light-headed. "I'm feeling kind of done."

"Come on, not yet," Simon said. "There's more to explore."

Jade pulled out her phone. "I don't have any signal, and it's almost lunchtime. I think we should head back."

Simon sighed. "The rock is probably blocking cell reception, but let's go a little further." He held the flashlight under his chin so it cast his face in an eerie glow. In a creepy voice, he said, "I promise no harm will befall you."

Jade laughed nervously. "You're such a dork."

They continued deeper into the cave until the tunnel ended at a stone wall. Simon swung his flashlight across the floor with a sigh. "I really thought we'd find something."

From somewhere in the blackness around them came a low, rumbling growl.

"Please tell me that was you," Jade whispered.

Simon swallowed a sudden lump in his throat. "Um . . . that would be no."

"Okay, I'm freaking out here," Jade said. "I really think we should—"

As Simon pointed the flashlight at a rocky shelf, a huge shape hurtled toward them out of the darkness.

CHAPTER 6

THE TWINS screamed.

Large round eyes in a giant feline shape gleamed in the light. The creature rushed at them, and Simon stumbled backward, sending the flashlight beam swinging wildly. With no time to run, Jade threw her hands up and braced for impact.

It never came. In a flash, the creature was past them, running lightly on the slick floor toward the cave entrance. Simon thrust the flashlight at the retreating creature, but it was already gone.

"Come on!" he yelled, racing back the way they'd come.

Jade hesitated, her terror of getting closer to the creature battling with her intense desire to flee the cave. Her craving for sunshine and open air won out. She hurried after Simon, trying not to slip.

Rounding the bend in the tunnel, they saw the creature silhouetted in the light of the entrance. It was low to the ground, crouching on all fours. A growl rolled toward them once again. Simon halted, a sob rising in his throat as he realized it was blocking their escape.

The twins stood side by side, unsure of what to do. Sunlight and freedom were so close, yet felt impossibly distant. Simon's hand found Jade's, and she returned his tight grip.

As their eyes adjusted to the sudden brightness coming from the cave opening, the creature shifted and moved into the light.

Jade and Simon froze, staring intently.

Then Simon's shoulders relaxed, and he blew out a long breath. Jade groaned, her hand coming to her forehead, before doubling over with relief. Was the creature dangerous? Sure. A monster? Hardly.

Standing before them was a bobcat, three and a half feet long, with thirty pounds of fur and muscle. It loped off through the trees and disappeared. The twins looked at each other, color slowly returning to their pale cheeks. Simon flashed Jade an embarrassed grin. She scowled back, but couldn't hold it and broke into a rueful laugh.

They walked out of the cave, squinting in the late-morning light. "I'm going to make a wild guess and say that was *not* Panther Man," Jade said.

"Nope. But why did it look so huge back in the cave?"

"It must have been the way the flashlight hit

it, making its shadow way bigger than the actual animal."

Simon looked thoughtful. "You know, just because we didn't find Panther Man doesn't mean he doesn't exist."

"Come on, Simon, there was nothing there. No bones, no footprints. Not even a panther-sized couch and TV."

"Hilarious," Simon said. "People are seeing *something*. And I'm going to find out what it is."

CHAPTER 7

WHEN THE twins came out for breakfast the next morning, Henri's room was empty. They ate at the small table off the kitchen before heading down the creaking stairs. Not finding their grandpa in the office or the gift shop, they wandered into the museum.

In the medieval room, they saw Henri shifting old books in a large cabinet, examining each one carefully before setting it aside.

"Morning, Grandpa," Jade called.

Henri quickly closed the cabinet and turned to them with a smile. "Hey, kids. Didn't expect you up this early."

"Are you looking for something?" Simon asked. "Maybe we can help."

"No, no," Henri said. "Just reorganizing."

Jade glanced at the cabinet behind him. "Do you have any books on magic here? I found a cool one at the Raven last night."

Henri frowned. "No. No magic books. Now, why don't you two start cleaning? I'll open up and work the cash register."

Simon and Jade gathered their cleaning supplies and began working their way through the sprawling museum, dusting the displays and sweeping the wood floors. Visitors trickled in throughout the morning, but the crowd was light. When the twins entered a room at the back of the museum, they stopped short.

"Whoa!" Simon said, his voice tinged with awe.

Against the far wall stood a stuffed creature unlike anything they'd ever seen. It stood upright on a small wooden platform, towering a full seven feet in height. Its hyenalike face was frozen in a snarl, and its slump-shouldered, muscular frame was covered in short golden fur with reddish-brown spots. A spiky ridge of bristling red hair ran down its humped back. The monster's arms hung to its knees, with its fingers ending in long claws.

"What is *that*?" asked Jade.

"It looks like a werehyena," Simon said.

"That's a thing? I've heard of werewolves but never werehyenas."

"Shape-shifting monsters are based on lots of different animals." He read a small sign sitting on the platform at the monster's feet. *"The Morgund. A werehyena from Catonian mythology."*

"It's so lifelike," Jade said, peering up at the creature. "How'd they make it?"

"It's a lot more convincing than the Fiji mermaid," Simon said. "That was a big hoax in a museum a long time ago. Somebody sewed the top half of a monkey to the bottom half of a fish. Sounds ridiculous now, but it fooled a lot of people. I've got to ask Grandpa about this!"

They hurried to the gift shop, where Henri was handing a bag of souvenirs to a visiting couple.

"Why didn't you tell me about the morgund?" demanded Simon when the couple left. "It is *so cool*! Where'd you get it?"

Henri adjusted a postcard display beside the register. "At an estate auction recently. It's rare and expensive, so stay away from it. I'll clean it myself."

He looked at his watch. "Why don't you two go have lunch somewhere, my treat?" After handing Jade some money, he walked into his office.

Simon stared after him, disappointment etched on his face. "I want our old grandpa back. He used to love telling me *every detail* about a new exhibit. What's going on with him?"

"He's probably worried about the museum but doesn't want to talk about it. Mom said he and Grandma couldn't afford to hire extra help. If that werehyena was expensive, it probably made their money problems even worse." Jade sighed. "Come on, I'll let you pick the lunch place. As long as it's Poutine Palace."

They wove their way through the crowds along the boardwalk to the restaurant. After ordering at the counter, they snagged a table near the window and ate their poutine, plates of french fries covered in delicious gravy and cheese curds.

After taking a last satisfying slurp of her blueberry milkshake, Jade saw the headline on a stack of free local papers near the door. Her stomach sinking, she grabbed a copy and brought it to their table.

"Oh no," she said after scanning the front page. "There's an article about the creature sightings!"

"So much for keeping it out of the news," Simon said. "Must have been too tempting a story for the editor to leave out. What's it say?"

Jade read for a few moments. "Nothing much. It talks about the recent break-ins and wonders if they're related to reports of a large creature wandering downtown at night. No clear description other than that it walks upright." She frowned. "That's weird. I don't know of any large animals in Maine that walk on two legs."

"Hmmm," Simon said, tapping his lips with a mock-serious expression. "A big creature that walks upright around here? Gosh, what could it be?"

Jade rolled her eyes. "I know you're the president of the Panther Man fan club, but be serious." She kept reading. "The mayor says the incidents are unrelated and everything's under control. I hope this whole thing blows over and doesn't hurt attendance at the museum."

"I definitely don't want anything to mess up Grandpa's business," Simon said. "But wouldn't it be *awesome* if there really was a monster in Skull Rock?"

Jade smirked at her brother. "I'm going with *no*." She checked the time. "Come on, we should get back."

The rest of the afternoon passed uneventfully. After the museum closed, Henri made spaghetti, and they played Parcheesi. It was Jade's favorite board game, but Henri seemed distracted. He kept missing chances to send their pieces back to home.

That night, Jade tried to talk with her brother as

they lay in the dark, but he just mumbled a few responses before lightly snoring. She stayed awake, anxious about the news article and what it might mean for the museum. Finally, she drifted off to sleep.

Shortly after midnight, Jade's eyes shot open. Something had jolted her awake. Across the room, Simon continued snoring. Hearing nothing else, she was about to roll over when a low growl drifted up from the museum. It rose and fell in an ominous wave.

Jade threw her pillow at Simon.

"Wha?" he mumbled. "Wha's happening?"

"Shhh!" Jade hissed. "Listen!"

The growl came again, a rumble that grew to a roar like a chain saw. With a terrifying swell, it morphed into what sounded like the sharp brays of a strangled donkey. Jade pulled her knees protectively to her chest and clasped her hands over her ears. Simon grabbed his phone and scrambled to open his voice memo app, but before he could start recording, the spine-tingling noise died away, leaving an eerie silence in its wake.

The twins stared at each other, wide-eyed and pale.

Simon's voice trembled. "Did that sound like a creaking building to you?"

CHAPTER 8

THE DOWNTOWN clock above Skull Rock Mutual Bank read 1:27 a.m. Oceanside Lane, so bright and cheerful during the day, was shrouded in thick fog drifting in from the water. The mist swirled sluggishly in the breeze, creating eerie shapes in the moonlight.

A very different shape slipped through the shadows like a wraith, moving silently along the boardwalk. The tips of the beast's ears nearly brushed the hanging signs advertising the various shops. It paused in front of the window of the Sandman Sweets & Treats. The muted glow from a nearby streetlamp cast the beast's dim reflection in the glass. Huge. Muscular. Menacing. The monster sniffed, and its black lips curled in a satisfied snarl.

Moving to the door, it placed a fur-covered hand on the knob. With a sharp twist and a groan of metal, the beast snapped off the handle. It slammed one shoulder against the door, popping it open and causing a bell to jangle inside. Stepping through the doorway, the beast tore down the bell and tossed it aside. Its keen red eyes pierced the gloom as it moved easily through the dark shop.

It stopped at a row of clear plastic containers, each with a metal scoop attached to a cord. The sweet aromas of multicolored taffies, sea salt caramels, and delicate chocolate truffles filled the creature's nostrils. Tearing away a cover, the monster thrust its muzzle into a container and began to feed.

CHAPTER 9

"YOU LOOK as bad as I feel," Simon said to Jade when they woke the next morning.

"Thanks," Jade replied through a yawn. Neither of them had slept well after hearing the noise in the museum. They'd decided not to wake Henri again, thinking he might be more receptive in the morning.

"So what do you think of my Panther Man theory now?" Simon asked. "That did kind of sound like a panther scream."

Jade frowned. "I don't know what to think. Even if it was Panther Man, why is it breaking into places? Why the museum?"

"No idea," Simon said. "But if it broke in, maybe we can find evidence."

They made their way to the dining area. Henri was sitting at the small table reading the newspaper with a grave expression. Folding it quickly, he looked up with a tight smile. "Morning. How'd you sleep?"

"Not great," Simon said. "We heard the noise again."

Henri's smile faltered. "I'm sorry the building sounds are bothering you. You'll get used to them."

"I don't think it was the building," Jade stressed. "The growl was louder this time."

"And turned into some kind of donkey scream," Simon said.

Henri's lips pursed in a tight line. "That's . . .

interesting. I'll keep an eye out for anything un-usual, but I'm sure it's nothing."

Jade glanced at Simon. "Um . . . that scream wasn't nothing, Grandpa."

"Yeah, it was pretty much the opposite of noth-ing," Simon said.

Henri met the twins' serious expressions for a moment before staring out the window. "Right. Okay, I'll have a look around downstairs, but try not to worry. Have some breakfast. I'll meet you in the museum." Tucking the paper under his arm, he strode from the room and headed downstairs.

"What's going on with him?" Simon asked, the hurt evident in his voice. "Why won't he believe us?"

Jade frowned. "And how could he not hear that noise? Maybe he needs new hearing aids."

The twins ate croissants and blueberry yogurt mixed with granola. After washing the dishes, they headed downstairs and examined all the windows and doors. There was no sign of a break-in.

They fell into their routine of prepping the museum for the day. While restocking the gift shop, Simon spotted the newspaper Henri had been reading lying near the cash register. He slipped the paper under his shirt and motioned for Jade to follow him into the museum.

When they were alone, Simon held up the newspaper. "I want to know what Grandpa was reading about." He scanned the front page as Jade crowded close.

"There have been more creature sightings!" Simon whispered excitedly.

Jade scanned the article. "Better description this time—tall with golden fur. Isn't Panther Man supposed to have black fur?"

Simon's forehead wrinkled. "Yeah. Panther Man sightings always report him having black fur, so that doesn't fit at all." A moment later, his face brightened. "But think about it—the report doesn't say black or brown fur like most wild animals—it says golden. Even if it's not Panther Man, it *must* be a monster!"

Jade sighed. "Just because we don't know what it is yet doesn't mean it's a monster."

As Simon chewed his lip thoughtfully, his eyes widened. "Hey, you know what else is tall and golden? The *morgund*."

"Yeah. So?"

"We've been hearing those weird sounds in the museum, right? What if the sightings and the sounds are related?"

"Are you suggesting that a stuffed museum exhibit is taking nightly strolls around the neighborhood?" Jade asked, her eyebrow arching.

"When you say it like that, it sounds ridiculous," Simon said. "So don't say it like that."

"How would *you* say it?"

"You've gotta admit, the description sounds a lot like the morgund. I think we should follow this lead."

"There *is* no lead," Jade said. "The morgund is a statue of a made-up animal! It's not *alive*."

"So that freaky donkey howl was just the building creaking?" Simon asked.

"Well, no, of course not. I don't know what it was, but that doesn't mean it's the morgund."

"Wouldn't you do *anything* to save the museum?" Simon said. "Even if there's only a small chance of helping Grandpa, shouldn't we take it?"

Jade hesitated. "I guess so. What are you thinking?"

Simon grinned. "Ever been on a stakeout?"

CHAPTER 10

"THIS IS a bad idea," Jade whispered to Simon as they set the table for dinner.

"Why didn't you say so before?" Simon asked.

"I'm saying it now." She looked uncomfortable. "What about the security alarm? We'll set it off if we're wandering the museum at night."

Simon crossed his arms. "First of all, we won't be *wandering*. We're doing a stakeout. Secondly, if there really was an alarm, whatever's been in the museum would have set it off. I think Grandpa said that to keep us from sneaking around."

Henri entered from the kitchen with a plate full of burgers. "All right, dinner's up. I know it's not fancy." He glanced down. "Sophie's the better cook."

"Will she be home soon?" Jade asked. "How's Aunt Geneviève?"

He set the plate on the table. "It might be a while. Sophie's got her hands full at the moment."

"That's okay, Grandpa," Simon said as he grabbed a burger. "I love your food."

Over dinner, Henri asked the twins about their friends and how they felt about going into seventh grade. Jade and Simon got him to tell stories about growing up in a small riverside town in southern France. After doing the dishes, they played Rook, a card game Henri had loved since he was young.

"Yes!" Simon said as he laid his final card with a flourish. "I finally beat you, Grandpa!"

"Looks like I taught you too well." Henri chuckled.

Sensing Henri's positive mood, Simon asked, "Can you tell us more about the morgund? Like where you got it and everything? It's really cool."

Henri paused, his expression conflicted. "I don't mean to be evasive about the morgund, but it's hard to explain why it's special to me."

"You said earlier that it was rare and expensive," Jade said.

Henri nodded. "Yes, but it's more than that." He stared at the ceiling as if searching for the right words. "Ever since I was younger than you two, I've been fascinated by the mysteries of the world, by strange, unexplained things. I wanted to explore them, understand them, and share them with other people. That's why I started this museum. It's my life's work. The morgund is the perfect symbol of all of that. It represents everything I love." He glanced down at his weathered hands. "That probably sounds silly."

"No, I get it," Simon said. "Really."

Henri gave the twins a somber look. "I might as well tell you the last part. I don't want you to worry, but business hasn't been great lately. I bought the morgund hoping it becomes a big draw for the museum and helps turn things around. So you can see why I'm possessive and want to take care of it myself."

Jade squeezed Henri's hand. "Of course, Grandpa. I'm sorry things are stressful."

"Yeah, thanks for telling us," Simon said.

Henri nodded. "I think it's time to turn in. For all of us. Straight to bed, you two, all right? Good night."

When Henri's door closed behind him, Jade said, "Wow, that was a lot. Poor Grandpa." She glanced nervously at Simon. "Are we still doing this?"

"We have to, for his sake," Simon said. "If he can't face that something's going on, then we'll do it for him. But let's wait till he's asleep. I don't want him to hear us on the creaky steps."

Forty-five minutes later, Simon poked his head out their bedroom door. "Grandpa's light's out," he whispered. "Let's go."

With their blankets and pillows, the twins padded quietly across the living room, through the security door, and down the steps. Jade paused at the bottom. Even with Simon's assurances, she was still nervous about the alarm. He pushed past her into the gift shop and shook his backside randomly. "Look, I'm doing the Butt Dance. See? No alarm."

She fought the grin tugging at her lips. "How can *my* twin be such a horrible dancer?"

They entered the museum. Already spooky during the day, it was genuinely scary at night. Red light from emergency exit signs cast an eerie glow over the displays, creating deep shadows and strange silhouettes. The giant hanging crocodile seemed to follow them with its glass eyes. Jade imagined the animal skulls were laughing at her for daring to venture into their dark domain. Carved wooden creatures that were normally just interesting now looked terrifying. She shivered in the deep silence.

"It's so creepy," she whispered.

"Yeah, isn't it great?" Simon said.

He led them along the aisles to the back room where the morgund was displayed and stopped short. A pair of large wooden pocket doors blocked the entrance. "What's with these doors?" Simon stepped forward and tried to pull them open. "Locked. Since when does Grandpa close parts of the museum at night?"

"Maybe he's worried about the break-ins. He did say the morgund was really valuable."

"There goes our stakeout," Simon said gloomily.

"Not necessarily," Jade said.

"What do you mean?"

She flashed him a grin. "I'm a magician, remember?"

Jade hurried to the gift shop and grabbed two large paper clips from a box below the cash register. Back at the door to the morgund room, she shined her phone's flashlight at the lock. Nodding in satisfaction, she began bending the paper clips into new shapes.

"How exactly did you learn this?" Simon asked.

"One of my magic books has a chapter on picking simple locks. It can help with illusions and escape tricks and stuff."

She inserted one clip into the lock and applied gentle pressure, then slid the second one in above it. After moving the second clip around for a minute, Jade heard a click. She tugged on the doors, and they rolled open.

"I'm impressed," Simon said.

Jade slipped the paper clips into her pocket as they stepped through the doorway. The towering morgund looked even more menacing in the gloom. Watery moonlight filtering through a nearby window glinted off the werehyena's long fangs. Swallowing the lump in her throat, Jade helped Simon spread their blankets in the aisle at the monster's feet.

She eyed the backpack he plopped between them. "What's this?"

"Stakeout supplies," he said and began pulling out items. "Flamin' Hot Doritos, Peanut M&M'S, Frappuccinos, card games, and horror comics."

"Horror comics?" Jade asked, her nose wrinkling. "We're camped out in a creepy museum at night in front of a werehyena. Isn't that scary enough?"

"I'm a true fan," Simon said, tearing open the Doritos bag.

Jade gazed around the spooky room as she munched on a chip. In one corner stood a forest scene with a cutout of Bigfoot in the familiar striding pose from the famous 1967 video recording. Water ran down an artificial rock face and filled a small pool. *Even water sounds scary in this place,* Jade thought. "So what do you think's going to happen?"

"Probably nothing," said Simon. "But at least we'll have eliminated one possibility of what people are seeing."

"I hope you're right, but I'm a little freaked out. I mean, those noises *were* pretty scary."

"I'm nervous too," Simon admitted. "But how often do you get the chance to investigate a *real* spooky mystery? Come on, I'll let you beat me at Exploding Kittens."

The twins played cards and ate snacks until Jade's eyelids began to droop. Even drinking Frappuccinos couldn't keep her awake, and she was too tired to be scared anymore.

"Get some sleep," Simon said, picking up a comic. "I'll take first watch."

"Okay," Jade said through a yawn. "Wake me up if anything happens or you get sleepy." She fluffed her pillow and snuggled under her blanket with her back to the morgund. In seconds, she was asleep.

Twenty minutes later, Simon's snores echoed softly through the dark museum. Neither twin was watching for a monster.

But a monster was watching them.

CHAPTER 11

SIMON WOKE to the sound of Jade's fart.

"Gross," Simon said, managing to wrinkle his nose and yawn at the same time.

"Everybody farts," Jade mumbled. "If we didn't, we'd explode."

They sat up and stretched their aching muscles. "I'm never gonna complain about a mattress again," Simon said. A clump of his hair stood up like a rooster's comb.

Jade nodded sleepily. "Nice hairstyle."

"Thanks. It's all the rage in Paris." He turned off the phone alarm he'd set the night before and looked up at the morgund, standing unmoved in the early-morning light. "Well, there goes that theory."

"It was worth a shot," Jade said, gathering up her blanket and pillow. "Come on, let's get back upstairs before Grandpa catches us."

After locking the morgund room's door behind them, the twins eased their way up the creaking steps. They collapsed on their beds and immediately fell asleep.

All too soon, they were awakened by a knock on their door. "Come on, sleepyheads," Henri called. "I made pancakes."

A few minutes later, the twins plopped down at the table.

"Aren't you two a bundle of energy this morning," Henri said, setting down his iPad.

"Mmph," Simon muttered, dragging a stack of pancakes onto his plate.

Jade gave Henri a weak thumbs-up.

"I see now is not the time for conversation," Henri said. "I'll meet you downstairs after your brains catch up to your bodies." He rose and playfully flattened Simon's hair before leaving the room.

Simon revived over the warm, fluffy pancakes. "He seems in a better mood."

Jade nodded, looking thoughtful. She picked up the iPad Henri had left on the table and scrolled for a few moments. "He was reading local news updates. There's nothing about creature sightings or break-ins last night."

"And no noises either," Simon added. "Strange that it was quiet the night we did the stakeout."

Jade's brow furrowed. "Yeah. Strange."

CHAPTER 12

JADE AND Simon stumbled through the day's work at the museum. After a dinner of frozen pizza, they watched an old movie called *The Princess Bride* with Henri. Exhausted from their stakeout the previous night, the twins slept soundly.

When Simon woke the next morning, he opened the local news app he'd installed on his phone. A minute later, he sat up, his eyes wide. "Jade!"

"Not so loud. You're disturbing my Zen."

Simon came over and sat on the edge of her bed. "Your Zen is about to be wrecked—there was another store break-in on Oceanside Lane last night. And the security camera caught this." He turned his phone screen toward Jade. A blurry black-and-white photo showed an upright figure striding away from the camera. It was tall and light-colored with what appeared to be a dark line running down its back.

Jade sat up quickly. She took the phone and zoomed in on the image. "Simon, this looks like—"

"The morgund," he finished.

"But how?" Jade said. "I mean, nothing happened when we did the stakeout."

"Maybe nothing happened *because* we did the stakeout."

Jade bit her lip. "We need to talk to Grandpa."

They dressed hurriedly and went to the kitchen.

Henri sat at the table, gazing out the window with a solemn expression. His iPad lay beside him.

"Grandpa?" Simon said.

Henri shook his head slightly as if coming back from a faraway place and turned toward them. "Sorry, kids. My mind was somewhere else."

"That's okay," Jade said. "But we need to talk to you."

"What about?" Henri asked.

Simon swallowed a lump in his throat. "The morgund." Henri looked wary, but Simon pushed ahead. "We know how much it means to you, but a security camera captured something during a break-in last night, and well . . . look." He held out his phone.

Henri's cheek twitched. He looked away and cleared his throat. "I read about the break-in this morning, but I don't see what that has to do with the morgund."

"But, Grandpa," Jade said, "this photo looks a lot like—"

"That photo doesn't look like much to me," Henri interrupted. "It could be anything. Any*one*, I mean." He stood. "You kids have been spending too much time in this spooky old museum, and these supposed sightings are playing with your imaginations. Why don't you take the day off? We restocked yesterday, and I can handle the register. Forget about the morgund and this creature nonsense. Be kids. Have fun. I'll see you later." He left the room and walked down to the museum.

Jade sighed. "That went well."

Simon stared after Henri. "What is *up* with him? I mean, I get that he's worried about the museum, but it's more than that. It feels like he's hiding something."

"He obviously doesn't want to talk any more about the morgund or the sightings, but I don't know why."

Simon set his jaw. "Then we'll just solve this mystery ourselves."

After a quick breakfast, the twins sat on Simon's bed while Jade opened her laptop and typed "werehyenas" into the search engine.

"That one is so cool!" Simon said, pointing to a painting of a hyena monster.

"Not the word I'd use for it," Jade said, wrinkling her nose at the gruesome image.

"Plenty of entries," Simon noted as Jade scrolled through the search results. "Looks like lots of countries have werehyena myths."

She clicked on various links. "Heightened hearing and agility," Jade murmured as she read. "Fast and powerful with strong jaws."

"Hates fire, active only at night, and vulnerable to silver like a werewolf," Simon said, his eyes scanning the screen.

"Hey, the females are bigger and stronger than the males, and the natural leaders of werehyena packs." She nudged her brother. "Maybe I should become a werehyena. Then I could boss you around."

"As if I'd listen. I *am* eleven minutes older."

"You might not have a choice. Says here that all female werehyenas do magic. I could put you under my spell." She waved her fingers in front of his face. "Wow, this is, like, my dream monster."

Simon pushed her hand away. "See? I told you monsters were cool. Now look up the morgund."

Jade tapped the keys and read aloud, *"The morgund is a werehyena from Catonian mythology. Created by dark magic, it was greatly feared by villagers across Catonia for its savage practice of eating children."*

"Eating *children*?" Simon said. "That's pretty brutal, even for me."

They continued searching the internet without

finding anything else that felt relevant. Jade closed her laptop with a sigh. "We got some interesting info, but I don't see how it helps us."

Simon chewed his lip. "We have to know if the morgund is actually moving."

"It didn't move during the stakeout," Jade said.

"Maybe it sensed us somehow and didn't want to reveal itself."

"Too bad we're not invisible."

Simon grinned. "That's it. We'll be invisible."

"Come again?"

"We'll use the security system."

"But there's no alarm. You did the Butt Dance, remember?"

"True, but there *are* security cameras." Simon hopped off the bed. "Come on."

They headed downstairs and hurried to the morgund room. To their surprise, Henri was standing in front of the creature, gazing up at its fearsome face. As they approached, Jade thought she could hear him whispering something.

"Grandpa?" she said.

Henri turned quickly to face them. "Hey, kids. Didn't hear you there."

"What are you doing?" Simon asked.

Henri smoothed his thinning silver hair. "Just checking on my prize exhibit. Aren't you going outside? It's a nice day."

"Yeah," Simon said. "We just wanted to look around the museum for fun first. Don't always get the chance when we're working."

Henri nodded distractedly. "Speaking of working, I should get back to the register. Don't stay inside too long."

He slipped past the twins toward the gift shop. Simon raised an eyebrow at Jade, who simply shrugged. They gazed along the ceiling of the mor-gund room. In the far corner, a small security cam-era faced the door.

"Doesn't look like it would catch the morgund," Simon said.

"So let's move it," said Jade.

Simon stared at her. "Who are you, and what have you done with my sister?"

"You must be having a bad influence on me. Let's get the ladder."

They went to the supply closet, where a stepladder rested beside the mops and brooms. After Simon made sure Henri was nowhere in sight, Jade carried the ladder back to the morgund room. Placing it in the corner, she scrambled up and carefully reposi-tioned the security camera.

When the ladder was back in the closet, Simon rubbed his hands together excitedly. "Now let's see what we catch in our monster trap."

CHAPTER 13

LATER THAT night, the beast crouched motionless on a rooftop, moonlight reflecting off its golden fur. Its sensitive nostrils quivered as it sampled the banquet of smells floating on the ocean breeze.

A dog barked somewhere in the distance. The beast snapped its huge head to one side, peering in the direction of the sound. Saliva dripped from its lips as its stomach rumbled with hunger.

The beast slipped down the side of the building and raced into the night.

CHAPTER 14

THE NEXT morning, the twins bounded out of bed.

"We can't seem too excited," Jade warned. "We don't want Grandpa to get suspicious."

They dressed and walked to the dining table to find Henri holding his iPad with a stricken expression.

"Are you okay, Grandpa?" Jade asked.

Henri looked up, his face a storm of emotion.

Without a word, he stood and strode from the room. Moments later, the twins heard his heavy tread on the stairs.

Simon hurriedly opened his news app. Jade crowded next to him as they scrolled the headlines.

"Oh no!" Jade gasped. "It attacked someone!"

Simon read, his voice shaking, *"Last night, Isaac Washington, age fifty-five, was attacked by an unknown assailant while walking his dog near his home in Skull Rock. Authorities were led to the injured man by the dog, who was discovered alone and trailing its leash on Oceanside Lane. An unnamed police official reported that the injuries were consistent with an animal attack. This incident, combined with the rash of break-ins and reported creature sightings, will undoubtedly increase pressure on Mayor Thompson to offer real solutions before these events impact summer tourist season. An official statement is expected soon."*

Jade looked at Simon, her eyes wide. "But we didn't hear any growling last night. Why would the morgund start being quiet?"

Simon bit his lip. "Maybe it realized that making noise is what led to our stakeout."

"So you think the morgund is, like, aware? And smart?"

"I really hope not." Simon ran a hand through his thick black hair. "Let's check the security footage from last night."

They hurried down the stairs and peeked into the office. Henri wasn't there. In one corner sat a desktop computer. A digital recorder was plugged into it with a label that read ACE SECURITY.

"Where's Grandpa?" Jade asked. "We've got to make sure he doesn't catch us checking the recordings."

They slipped quietly into the museum and spotted Henri in a back room, leaning over a display case. A moment later, he repeated the motion with another case.

"What's he looking for?" Simon whispered.

Jade shook her head and motioned for them to retreat.

Back in the office, they stared at the security system. "This might take a few minutes," Jade said. "One of us better watch out for Grandpa."

"I'll do it," Simon said. "You're better with computers." He moved to the door, where he could look through the gift shop into the museum.

Jade hunched over the computer and examined the desktop. She clicked on various icons, trying to understand the interface.

"You'd better hurry," Simon whispered.

"Don't rush me!" Sweat pricked Jade's armpits. She clicked several more times until a black-and-white image of the gift shop appeared on the screen. "Room 1, Room 2," she muttered, navigating her way around the labels on the display. "There it is . . . June 11 . . ."

"Hey, Grandpa!" Simon said in an overly enthusiastic voice, stepping into the gift shop as he spotted Henri approaching. "I was looking for you. What do you want us to work on today?"

Henri frowned. "Oh, right. Um . . . just the usual cleaning and stocking. I'm going to work in my office until we open."

"Before you do that," Simon said quickly, "I was wondering if you could . . . um . . . show me how to work the cash register?"

Henri's brow furrowed. "I already showed you that. You were working it fine the other day."

"Yeah, but . . . uh . . . the drawer kept getting stuck," Simon said.

"It did?" Henri said. He walked over to the register and pressed a button. The drawer popped open.

"Wow, look at that," Simon said. "You fixed it! Good job, Grandpa."

"Are you all right?" Henri asked, giving Simon a suspicious look.

"Me? Sure! Never better."

"Me too, Grandpa," Jade said as she appeared beside Simon with a broad smile. "Ready to work!"

"Okay, great," Henri said with a puzzled expression. "I'll be in my office if you need me."

As he disappeared into the office, Jade pulled Simon into the museum.

"So?" Simon asked excitedly. "What'd you find?"

Her expression was grim. "There's no footage from the morgund room at all! A cable is missing from the back of the recorder. It must have been the one to the camera we moved." She ground her teeth in frustration. "We've got nothing."

"The one camera we need is the one that's not

working?" Simon blew out a frustrated breath, then frowned. "You don't think Grandpa might have unplugged it on purpose, do you?"

The twins stared at each other, their faces pale, neither of them saying what they were both thinking—their investigations into the mysterious break-ins and monster sightings were pointing to Grandpa Henri.

CHAPTER 15

TWENTY MINUTES later, the bell over the front door of the museum jingled. The twins heard a loud squawk and a deep voice call out, "Salut!"

Dustcloths in hand, the twins hurried over to find Jacques in the gift shop with Edgar perched on his shoulder.

"Hey, Jacques," Jade said. "What was that you said?"

"Salut," Jacques repeated. "It is a way to say hello in French."

Simon looked at the raven in surprise. "That's so cool you can take Edgar outside!"

Jacques glanced over at the bird. "He is too old and spoiled to fly away. Besides, in his mind, he is taking *me* for a walk. Is your grandfather here?"

"I am." Henri emerged from the office and shook hands with his friend. "What brings you by this morning?"

"We need to talk," Jacques said. "Did you hear about the attack last night?"

Henri looked grave. "Yes."

"This is not good," Jacques said. "Not for that poor man, not for any of us. There is no keeping this story contained now—it will spread. Already my business is down. People are scared."

Henri put up a restraining hand and said to the twins, "Why don't you two get back to cleaning. Jacques and I have, uh, business to discuss."

Edgar took flight and glided into the museum,

cawing loudly. As Henri took Jacques into his office, the twins went in search of the bird. Rounding a corner of the walkway, Jade peered into the next room. "Look!"

Edgar was perched on the morgund's head.

"What are the odds of that?" Simon said as they approached.

The raven cawed loudly and flew over to a red cabinet holding a display of Sasquatch footprints cast in plaster beside the artificial waterfall. He eyed the twins and squawked again.

"He sure is noisy today," Simon said.

"I'd be noisy too, seeing those huge footprints for the first time," Jade said. "They creep me out."

Turning back to the morgund, she studied the massive creature—the golden fur dotted with reddish spots. The bristling ridge of stiff hair running down its back. Its menacing snarl and long, blade-like claws . . .

Jade sucked in a startled breath. Spreading the fingers of her right hand wide, she touched them gently to the tips of the morgund's claws, measuring the distance between them. Keeping her fingers locked in that position, she grabbed Simon with her other hand and pulled him from the room, ignoring his grumbling.

Jade raced through the gift shop and pounded up the stairs with Simon at her heels. At the security door to Henri's apartment, she faced her brother and held up her hand.

"This is the distance between the morgund's claws." With that, she lifted her fingertips to the four parallel scratches in the door's paint that she'd noticed when they first arrived.

It was a perfect match.

CHAPTER 16

THE TWINS made their way slowly back to the morgund room and gazed up at the monster. Its large ruby-red eyes glared back at them.

"Simon, what is going on here?" Jade asked softly.

As Edgar resumed cawing, Jacques strode into the room. "Bird! Stop all that racket. Come. We have to open the shop." Edgar flew to Jacques's shoulder, and the man turned to the twins. "I am glad you are both here. Henri needs you right now, though he is too stubborn to admit it."

After Jacques left, they opened the museum. Worried Henri would dismiss the door marks matching the morgund's claws as a coincidence, the twins kept silent, dutifully working the cash register and cleaning the displays. By midafternoon, visitors were scarce. "Things are pretty slow here, Grandpa," Simon said as Henri emerged from his office. "Can Jade and I have the rest of the day off to wander downtown?"

Henri paused in his walk through the gift shop and looked around distractedly. "Uh . . . sure, why not? Just be back for dinner."

The twins hurried onto the boardwalk. "I know you," Jade said. "Where are we really going?"

"Where else?" Simon said with a gleam in his eye. "To talk to the one person we *know* has seen the monster."

Fifteen minutes later, Jade stared at the hospital looming above them. "Are you sure you know what you're doing?"

"Of course," Simon said. "Well, kind of. I have a plan, anyway."

"Which is?"

"If anyone asks, we're here to visit a sick relative."

"Who?"

"Uncle Isaac. That's the name of the guy who was attacked."

"But we don't have an uncle Isaac."

Simon rolled his eyes. "*They* don't know that, do they? Come on."

The twins entered the lobby and approached an information desk, where a middle-aged woman glanced up from a magazine. "Can I help you?"

"Um, yeah," Simon said. "We're here to visit Isaac Washington?"

The woman typed on a computer. Her eyes scanned the screen and widened in surprise. After a moment, she looked up at them. "How do you know Mr. Washington?"

"He's our uncle," Simon said smoothly.

The woman eyed them carefully. Finally, she shrugged and said, "Well, you're obviously not the press. Third floor, room 313."

Simon thanked her, and they headed for the elevators. Once inside, Jade said, "Did you catch what she said about the press? Sounds like we're not the only ones who had this idea."

When the door slid open, the twins moved past the nurses' station and followed the room numbers down the hall. The door to room 313 was open, and they peeked inside. An older man with hair twists lay on a bed, surrounded by softly beeping machinery. A nurse stood beside him adjusting dials and tapping on a digital pad. Jade took Simon's elbow and led him further down the hallway. They stood watching the door while trying not to look suspicious.

When the nurse left the room a minute later, the twins hurried forward and slipped inside. They hung back, looking at the man uncertainly. His eyes were closed, but he jerked fitfully as if in a fevered dream.

Jade poked Simon and nodded with her head toward the patient.

"This is weird," Simon whispered.

"It was your idea."

"I *know* that," he growled.

They moved to stand beside the bed. If the man noticed them, he made no sign. "Um . . . Mr. Washington?" Simon asked meekly.

The man's eyes fluttered open, and he stared at Simon with a glazed expression. "Tom?"

"No, sir. I'm Simon. We were wondering if we could ask you a few questions about the attack?"

"I'm so glad you're here, Tom," Mr. Washington said. "So glad." His speech was slurred, and his eyelids drooped. White bandages covered his arms and right cheek.

"Could you tell us what you saw last night?" Jade asked.

"Last night?" Mr. Washington said, his eyes darting around the room. "Dog. Charlie. Walking Charlie. Then . . ." Tears slid down his cheeks as his face contorted in fear. "*It* came." His voice was a ragged whisper.

"What was it?" Simon asked, leaning close. "What did you see?"

"So tall," Mr. Washington whispered, his brown skin glistening with sweat under the fluorescent lights. "Those big red eyes. And that sound. That horrible, horrible sound . . ."

"Yes?" Jade prompted. "What sound?"

The man shuddered. "Laughter. As it attacked me, it was . . . laughing."

CHAPTER 17

"THAT LOOK on his face is going to haunt me tonight," Jade said quietly as they walked back to the museum. "He was terrified just thinking about the attack."

"I feel bad we made him relive it," Simon said. "I thought if he didn't want to talk about it, he'd just tell us to leave. When he confused me with someone else, I didn't know what to do."

"We did learn about the laughing," Jade said. "That wasn't in the news reports."

Simon looked at her intently. "You know which animal is known for making laughing sounds, right?"

She swallowed hard. "Hyena."

The museum was closed when they arrived, so they let themselves in with the key Henri had given them. After climbing the steps, they looked around the empty living room and kitchen before heading to the open door of their grandpa's bedroom.

Henri sat at an old-fashioned rolltop desk with his back to the door. He was bent low over a book, staring at it intently. A stack of other ancient-looking books sat beside him.

"We're home, Grandpa," Simon said.

Henri stood quickly and pulled down the cover on the rolltop desk, hiding the books from view. "I didn't hear you come in. You startled me." Taking a key from his pocket, he locked the desk. "How was your afternoon?"

"It was . . . interesting," Jade said. "What are those books you were reading?"

"Oh, nothing important," Henri said. "Old history stuff. Hey, who's hungry? I'll get dinner started." He slipped past them and headed for the kitchen. Jade and Simon glanced at each other with matching raised eyebrows.

The next day, Henri took over the register at noon so the twins could get lunch on Oceanside Lane. Since the news report of the attack, the boardwalks were noticeably less crowded than when they'd first arrived in Skull Rock. Jade had started toward their favorite gourmet hot dog place when Simon grabbed her arm. "Let's go to the Raven."

"The Raven? Why?"

"We ran out of leads about the morgund online,

right? The Raven has rare books. Maybe there's one on Catonian history or something that mentions the morgund."

Jade nodded approvingly. "You're smarter than you look."

"You know we look a lot alike, right?"

"Not a chance. But let's hit Tasty Dog first. I need my food."

Simon had the Southwest Slammer Dog with bacon, cheddar cheese, and cactus relish while Jade polished off the Just-Like-Mama-Made Dog slathered in peanut butter and jelly. Pleasantly full, they hurried down the street to the Raven.

Jacques was behind the counter when they entered. "To what do I owe the pleasure? Is Henri with you?"

"Nope," Simon said. "We're on our lunch break. Just had Tasty Dog."

Jacques frowned and looked down at them through his gold-rimmed glasses. "Are your hands clean?"

The twins held up their hands for inspection, and Henri nodded. "All right. You may touch my books. Carefully."

"Always," Simon said. "Actually, we were wondering if you could help us find something."

Jacques removed his glasses and cleaned them on his shirt. "What do you wish to find? History? Cartography? Fine art? Architecture?"

"Do you have anything on the morgund?" Simon asked.

The old man gave them a quizzical look. "Morgund? I do not know this word. Is it English?"

Jade shrugged. "It's the name of a werehyena from Catonian mythology."

"Interesting. Why would you be researching such a thing?"

"Grandpa has a statue of one in the museum, and we thought it would be cool to learn more about it," Simon said.

"Très bon," Jacques said. "Henri was here looking for books on magic recently, perhaps for the same reason. Follow me." He headed for the back of the shop, stopping before the section Jade had discovered earlier with Edgar's help. "Option one, Mythology and Magic section. I do not know of this particular myth, but you may find something here. Also . . ." He pointed to another part of the shop. "History and Cultures section. There should be something on Catonia, which may help you. You will look. I will work. If you need me, call out 'Hé, vieil homme.'"

"What does that mean?" asked Jade.

"'Hey, old man,'" Jacques said with a wink, and walked away.

The twins pulled books from the shelves and

skimmed through chapter headings. "Anything interesting?" Simon asked twenty minutes later.

"These books are about magic and mythology—they're all interesting to me," Jade said. "But nothing on the morgund or Catonia."

Simon sighed. "Same here."

Edgar flew over and landed on the top shelf, cawing softly.

"Hey, Edgar," Jade said, glancing at her phone. "Lunch break's over. We should go."

Simon returned his book to the shelf. "We'll come back when we have more time. There have to be answers around here somewhere."

The twins said goodbye to Jacques and headed across the street to the museum. From the shop's window, Edgar watched them with a strangely intelligent look in his eyes.

CHAPTER 18

"YOUR CARD is . . . the three of diamonds!" Jade said triumphantly as she sat on her bed later that night.

Perched across from her, Simon raised an eyebrow. "Not even close. You're really bad at this."

"Urgh!" Jade said, throwing the playing cards on the bed in frustration. Half the deck slid over the edge onto the floor. "I wish Grandma were here to show me what I'm doing wrong. She's great at card tricks."

As she leaned over to pick up the fallen cards, Jade noticed a faint glow beneath her bed. "Hey, I can see light under here."

"That's weird," Simon said, kneeling down. "Where's it coming from?"

They pulled the bed away from the wall. The light seeped through a metal floor vent about a foot square in the corner of the room. "Shut off the lights," Simon said. "We'll be able to see better."

Jade flipped off their lamps, and they peered down through the vent.

"We can see right into the museum!" Simon said.

"Grandpa said this was an old building. They must have put in these kinds of vents for air flow or something back then. What room are we looking at?"

"Um . . . hard to tell with only the emergency lights on," Simon said. "Wait, there's that stool that's carved like a gargoyle."

Jade sucked in a breath. They'd cleaned the museum enough times to know where that stool was displayed.

"The morgund room!" they said simultaneously.

"This is why we've heard the noises at night so clearly!" Jade said. "They came right through this vent."

Simon's face lit up. "We can use this to spy on the morgund without being seen!" He shifted, trying to glimpse the werehyena through the grate. "The angle is wrong. I can only see one leg."

"That should be enough," Jade said.

He flashed her a grin. "Ready for another stakeout?"

After pushing Jade's bed against Simon's, they laid out their pillows and blankets on the floor beside the vent. Simon snuck to the kitchen and came back with snacks. They played Exploding Kittens in the glow of their phones' flashlights, keeping the room as dark as possible to help them see into the gloomy museum.

An hour and a half later, Jade yawned loudly. "I don't think I can—"

A low growl rumbled up through the vent, so soft they wouldn't have heard it in their sleep.

The twins froze, faces pale in the dim light. They quickly turned off their flashlights and pressed their eyes to the vent. Simon could just make out the morgund's leg at the edge of its display platform.

The leg moved. Its clawed foot stretched as if waking from a long sleep.

Jade gasped and clutched Simon's arm. She could feel him trembling. *I'm seeing a monster*, she thought, her mind caught in a dizzying swirl.

A whine drifted up through the vent as the morgund stepped off the platform and disappeared from view. After a metallic scrape came the sound of a window being pushed open. A few moments later, they heard it slide shut.

"Frozen toast, it really is the morgund!" Jade said. "What do we do?"

Simon bit his quivering lip. "We get proof. Come on!"

Grabbing her paper clip lockpicks, Jade followed Simon down the dark steps, staying close to the walls to minimize the creaking. At the bottom, Jade paused. "But . . . that thing is out there." Her voice broke, and she was shivering.

"We heard it leave, so we should be fine," Simon said, trying to convince himself as much as his sister. "And without proof, we'll never convince Grandpa or get him to tell us how he's involved in all this. Besides, it could keep hurting people."

Reluctantly, Jade nodded. They moved quietly through the gift shop and into the creepy museum, tiptoeing along the familiar route to the morgund room. Jade picked the lock and eased the doors slightly apart. Eyes to the crack, the twins peeked inside.

The morgund was gone.

Heart pounding, Simon entered the room with Jade at his heels and took a photo of the eerily empty platform. He gave a satisfied nod. "Now Grandpa will *have* to believe us!"

As they hurried back past the main entrance, the twins heard the distant sound of breaking glass. They froze, staring at the front door.

Jade's heart galloped like a stallion. "That sounded like it came from across the street."

Simon hesitated, then stepped toward the door.

"What are you doing?" Jade hissed.

"Just taking a look," Simon said. He tried to convince himself that his voice was shaking from excitement, but cold fear swept through him like a winter wind. After turning the lock, he slowly eased the door open and peered out. With a whimper, Jade stole up beside him and looked over his shoulder.

The streetlamps dotted Oceanside Lane with pools of light. The twins strained to see into the shadows cloaking the storefronts across the street.

"I don't see anything," Jade whispered.

"Me neither. I'm gonna check it out."

"Simon, no!"

Ignoring her, Simon slipped out onto the wooden boardwalk in front of the museum. He looked around carefully and motioned to Jade.

With a growl of frustration, she followed. "If I get killed, I'm coming back to haunt you."

Simon scurried forward and attempted to hide behind a too-small tree. Muttering in disgust, Jade pulled him down to crouch behind a large blue mailbox.

As Simon's eyes adjusted, he could see a jagged

hole in the front window of Skull Rock Toys & Teas, a popular tourist shop next door to the Raven. Was the monster inside? Or had it smashed the glass and moved on?

A flash of movement on the opposite boardwalk caught their eyes. Jade stiffened and tugged Simon's arm back toward the museum. He shook her off. Frightened as he was, this was his chance to finally see a real monster, and he wasn't going to miss it. With every nerve in his body tingling, Simon focused on the darkness near the broken window.

A creature darted into a pool of light. Simon gave an involuntary shriek, and Jade's nails dug into his arm.

They both slumped in relief as they recognized Toby, the store cat from Toys & Teas. He must have escaped through the broken window. Simon's relief quickly turned to disappointment. He'd really wanted to see the monster.

"Okay, we checked it out," Jade said as she stood. "The morgund's gone, so let's go tell Grandpa."

As Simon reluctantly turned to follow her, he noticed a sour, musky odor floating on the night breeze. "Hey, do you smell that?"

Before Jade could respond, a menacing growl rumbled in the darkness. With a squeak of fright, she bolted for the museum door. Simon broke out in a cold sweat, but stood trembling, trying to locate the source of the sound.

Glancing to one side, he saw a pair of large red eyes gleaming in the shadows beside a nearby streetlamp. On *his* side of the street.

The morgund stepped into the light.

Simon's scream froze in his throat. The towering beast's muscles rippled beneath its golden fur. Huge clawed hands curled into fists. The morgund lowered its head and glared at Simon, the movement highlighting the bristling ridge along its back.

Simon's dream of seeing a real monster had become a nightmare. Choking terror surged through him as he turned and fled to where Jade stood in the museum entrance, pleading for him to hurry. He hurtled inside as she slammed and locked the door.

They raced up the stairs and burst into Henri's room.

"Grandpa, wake up!" Simon said. "The morgund's alive!"

Groggily, Henri turned on his bedside lamp. "What? Why are you waking me up again?"

"We're sorry, but we had to," Jade said. "The morgund came to life and left!"

Henri's face set in an angry expression. "You went downstairs at night? I *told* you not to do that!"

"Because of the alarm?" Simon asked stubbornly. "The one that doesn't exist?"

Henri was momentarily silenced by the defiant stares of his grandchildren. He sighed. "All right, there is no alarm. I'm sorry I lied to you about that, but I didn't want to scare you with the real reason."

"Which is?" Jade asked.

"While I don't believe in this monster business, someone has been breaking into the shops on this street. That makes it dangerous for you two to be down in the museum at night." His expression softened into genuine concern. "What if something happened to you? What would your mother say? How could I live with myself if you got hurt?"

The twins looked at each other guiltily.

"Sorry, Grandpa," Simon said. "We get that, but the morgund is really gone! I've got a photo of the empty platform. I saw it in the street!"

"That's enough," Henri said. His expression hardened, and his voice was like ice. "I don't want to hear any more of your stories. Go to bed. We'll talk about this in the morning."

"But, Grandpa—" Jade began.

"Now!" Henri said.

The twins walked slowly back to their room, shocked by Henri's stubborn refusal to listen to them.

"What do we do?" Jade asked.

Simon shrugged helplessly, the hurt evident on his face. He fought to hold back tears. "We wait for the morgund to come back."

Jade's stomach sank. "Downstairs?"

Simon shook his head. "I think Grandpa's head would explode if he caught us down there now." He pointed to the grate in the floor. "We can try to video the morgund coming back. Even if we only catch its foot coming back on the platform, that will give us more proof to show Grandpa."

"But he didn't even want to look at the picture."

Simon's eyes narrowed. "We'll make him."

They settled down beside the grate. A few minutes later, they heard the bolt on the security door being quietly drawn back, followed by a stealthy tread on the creaking steps.

"Grandpa's going downstairs!" Simon whispered. "Does that mean he believes us?"

Jade tugged worriedly at her ponytail. "I don't know. Should we go too? I mean, what if the morgund comes back?"

"If Grandpa sees us, it will make everything worse. Maybe he's just checking out our story."

Jade nodded miserably, trying to block out the image of Henri coming face-to-face with a monster.

CHAPTER 19

"PASS ME another dog," James said. He glanced down the empty beach at the white gazebo in Skull Rock Park and shivered. In the late-night shadows, it looked like a mausoleum.

Freddie reached into a cooler and pulled out an uncooked hot dog. "Catch!" he said, throwing it at his friend.

The wet, slippery meat slid through James's fingers and fell to the ground. "Way to go, jerk."

Freddie laughed. "It's still good. The sand will give it some crunch."

Muttering, James grabbed another hot dog and slid it onto the end of his roasting stick. He held it over their campfire and gazed out at the ocean. The moonlight glowed off the whitecaps, creating a beautiful yet slightly eerie scene.

"Enjoy it while you can, man," Freddie said. "Another few months, and you'll be landlocked. Never understood why you want to go to college in Arizona." He scrunched up his nose. "Desert's got nothing on the ocean."

"NAU has a good design program," James said. "And it's in the mountains."

Over the rolling of the waves, James heard a low growl in the darkness behind him. Whipping his head around, he peered intently at the deep shadows cloaking the rocky cliff behind them. "Did you hear that growl?"

"A growl?" Freddie reached for a candy bar. "Nothing's growling out here but my stomach."

A patch of clouds shifted, momentarily bathing the cliff face in moonlight. A pair of large red eyes gleamed in a hulking silhouette seven feet above the sand. "What the . . . !" James exclaimed. "There's something out there! It's huge!"

Freddie looked where James was pointing as the clouds slid back over the moon. Seeing only shadows, he made a dismissive sound. "You're more scared than a little kid."

A pair of flashlights cut through the night, blinding the two boys. They squinted, shading their eyes with their hands. The flashlights lowered, and two police officers stepped into the firelight. "Evening, boys. What brings you out to the beach this late?"

"Just camping, officers," James said, motioning toward their sleeping bags. "We're going to spend the night."

"Sorry, fellas," the other officer said. "There's no

camping on public beaches. You can move over to one of the campgrounds down the road, though, okay? Make sure you douse that fire really well."

Freddie muttered something under his breath, but James said, "Will do. Sorry, we didn't know."

The officers nodded and started moving off. James looked nervously over his shoulder. The gleaming eyes were gone, but still . . .

"Wait for us!" James called out. "We'll come with you." Scrambling up, he used sand to smother the fire, then grabbed his sleeping bag and hurried to join the officers. Grumbling, Freddie followed.

Twenty feet away in the darkness beneath the cliff, the beast rose from its crouch and gazed after its prey, now retreating in a small pack. A disappointed growl rumbled in the monster's chest. It preferred isolated victims. Leaping up, it hooked its claws in the rugged rock face and climbed into the night to resume the hunt.

CHAPTER 20

"JADE, WAKE up!" Simon said, shaking her shoulder.

With a groan, Jade pushed herself off their bedroom floor and put a hand to her aching face. Grid lines from the vent were imprinted on her cheek. "What happened?"

"We fell asleep waiting for the morgund to come back," Simon said. "It's morning, and I can see its leg through the grate. Let's go look!"

"After we check on Grandpa."

The twins slipped quietly from their room and approached Henri's closed bedroom door. To their relief, they heard his bedsprings squeak as he rolled over, confirming his safe return. They made their way wearily down the stairs to the morgund room, where Jade unlocked the doors. The creature's fur glowed bronze in the sunlight streaming through a window as the werehyena stood in its usual position.

"I don't suppose last night was all a weird dream?" Jade asked.

Simon held up his phone displaying the picture of the empty platform. "Nope." He stepped tentatively closer to the morgund, peering up at its frozen snarl. "How could this thing just magically come to life?"

Jade chewed her lower lip. "Maybe magic *is* the answer. We read online that the morgund was created by some kind of dark spell."

"Does that mean there's an evil sorcerer running around Skull Rock or something?" Simon asked.

"Don't know. Grandpa said he got the morgund from an estate auction somewhere, but who knows if that's true."

Simon tugged at his pajama shirt. "I hate thinking that Grandpa's lying to us."

"Me too. But if he is, I'm sure he's got a good reason." Jade's face clouded—did she really believe that?

Simon opened the news app on his phone and groaned. "Another attack last night . . . the person's alive, but in the hospital . . . no photo . . . oh, please! The police are saying the attacks are by an aggressive black bear walking on its hind legs, and that they're working with animal control to capture and relocate it. The mayor is asking everyone to stay off the streets after dark. She says not to worry, as she's taking every precaution to ensure the safety of both residents and tourists."

"That's ridiculous!" Jade exclaimed. "The creature in that earlier photo was light colored and *clearly* not a bear. Besides, bears don't laugh while they shred you."

They headed upstairs and found Henri just sitting down at the table with a bowl of oatmeal. He looked up in surprise and shifted uncomfortably. "You two are up early."

"And you were up late," Simon said. "We heard you go downstairs last night. Did you see the morgund platform?"

Henri sighed wearily. "I didn't go downstairs to check on your story. After you woke me up, I couldn't sleep, so I went to work in my office for a while."

Simon clenched his jaw in frustration. "Well,

how do you explain this?" He held up the photo of the empty platform.

Henri squinted at the screen, and his face paled. "What . . . what's this all about?"

"The *morgund*," Simon said. "Like we said last night. Like we've been trying to tell you for days. I know it sounds totally unbelievable, but the morgund is coming to life at night. *That's* what everyone is seeing. *That's* what's doing the break-ins and attacking people!"

Henri's mouth worked silently for a few moments. "But . . . but that's preposterous. It's . . . it's stuffed, a fake . . ."

"Then how do you explain that photo, Grandpa?" Jade asked. "We're telling the truth. The morgund was *gone*, and now it's back!"

Henri's eyes darted around the room as if the answer could be found written on a wall. An uncomfortable silence filled the room. Then he stood suddenly, knocking his chair back. "This is *my* house, and you have to live by *my* rules! I'm telling you to stay in your room at night and keep away from that creature! Do you understand?" He trembled, his face flushed.

They stared at him in shock. Jade nodded and whispered, "Yes, Grandpa."

With a final glare at the twins, Henri stormed into his bedroom and slammed the door.

CHAPTER 21

"ARE YOU . . . okay?" Jade quietly asked her brother.

Simon had been unusually quiet since their fight with Henri earlier that morning. He sniffed, shifting listlessly on the park bench near the gazebo. "It's just . . . Grandpa and I always talked about the spooky stuff in the museum. That was our thing, like you and Grandma with magic. Now he's shutting me out and maybe even lying." He looked at

Jade, eyes bloodshot from crying. "Why won't he believe us?"

Jade gazed at the ground and nudged Simon's foot with her shoe. She hated seeing her brother like this. While she loved their grandpa, Simon was closer to him, as she was with Grandma Sophie. Her not being here was harder on Jade, and Henri's behavior was more difficult for Simon. "I don't know. Maybe he's too stressed to face another problem, especially when it's about something that means so much to him."

"But if he doesn't, these attacks are going to keep happening, and the museum could close. Then what's he going to do?" Simon picked up a pine cone and threw it toward the ocean in frustration.

Jade blew out a long breath. "We'll . . . figure something out."

The day crawled by like a sloth. As it was Monday

and the museum was closed, Jade and Simon didn't have their normal work to distract them. Henri and the twins mostly avoided each other—he holed up in his office doing paperwork, while they hung out at the beach.

That night, the twins set the table while Henri cooked dinner. He seemed to be banging pans more than usual, and the smell of burnt food filled the apartment. They ate in tense silence. Jade tried to start conversations a few times, but Henri's responses were brusque and short. Simon pushed food around his plate and didn't say anything.

Finally, Henri stood abruptly. "I'm going for a walk. You kids take care of the dishes, all right?"

"We could go with you," Jade said.

"No," Henri said firmly. After a pause, he added more softly, "Thanks, but I need to be alone for a while."

After Henri left, Simon said, "I don't know how

much more of this I can take. I mean, he won't even look at us! What do we do?"

Jade bit her lip. "We follow him."

"But he said he wanted to go out alone."

"I didn't hear the front door of the museum close."

Simon wrinkled his forehead. "You don't think he left?"

The twins slipped downstairs as quietly as the creaking steps would allow and moved through the eerily silent museum. The giant hanging crocodile seemed to grin at them with its rows of jagged teeth. Rounding a corner, they saw the door to the morgund room was closed for the night. On a hunch, Jade silently approached and placed one ear against the heavy wood. A soft murmuring came from inside. It rose and fell in a strange rhythm, but she couldn't make out the words.

She locked eyes with Simon, who had his own

ear to the door. After a few minutes, they snuck back to the apartment.

"What is Grandpa doing locked up with the morgund?" Simon asked. "I mean, I know it means a lot to him, but that's weird."

"It shouldn't wake up for hours yet, so at least he's safe." Jade rubbed her aching temples. "We need a new place to look for clues, but where?"

"We could try the Raven again, but it's closed for the night," Simon said.

Jade nodded distractedly as she glanced around the apartment. When her eyes fell on the closed door to Henri's bedroom, she caught her breath. "The books."

"What books?" Simon asked.

"The ones Grandpa was looking at in his room."

Simon's expression brightened. "I don't like snooping in his stuff, but if it helps us figure out what's going on with him, it's worth it." A moment later, his face fell. "But the books are locked in his desk, and Grandpa put the key in his pocket." He eyed his twin meaningfully. "Think you can . . . ?"

"Let's find out," she replied.

In Henri's bedroom, Jade pulled out her lock-picks and bent over the rolltop desk. A minute later, the wooden slats of the desktop cover rolled away to reveal the pile of books.

"You're handy to have around," Simon said.

"Let's hurry. We don't know when Grandpa will come back."

They each grabbed a book and started flipping through it. The volumes were bound in worn black or brown leather, and some had tarnished metal fastenings.

"These look really old," Jade said.

"This one's not in English."

"Eww. Mine's got creepy pictures."

"Let me see!" Simon said eagerly, crowding close.

Around the flowing, handwritten script were draw-ings of monsters attacking humans with their teeth and claws. "Cool," Simon breathed.

Jade drew a sharp breath. "These books are about magic! Dark magic, by the look of it. And Grandpa told me earlier there were no magic books in the museum."

"Technically these aren't in the museum."

"Close enough. He's been hiding these for a rea-son." Jade picked up another heavy book. "If some-one used dark magic to create the morgund, maybe we could find the spell or something. Look at the table of contents for anything about the morgund or werehyenas or Catonia."

They worked their way through the stack with-out any luck.

"I wish we could take these back to our room to study," Jade said.

"Grandpa would lose it if he found them missing. We can't risk it."

"Do you think we should call Mom and Dad about all this?"

Simon frowned. "I thought about it, but they've already left on their anniversary trip. If we tell them what's really going on, they'll probably freak out and leave early. They'll make us go home. I hate how things are between us and Grandpa right now, but I wanna stay and help him save the museum."

"Me too. And stop these attacks. We're the only ones who know about the morgund." She sighed. "I just wish we weren't on our own."

Simon cracked a slight smile. "Maybe we're not."

CHAPTER 22

THE NEXT morning, Jade and Simon emerged from their bedroom to find Henri sitting at the table. It was loaded with a platter of bacon, scrambled eggs, a huge stack of waffles, a bowl of strawberries, a bottle of maple syrup, and some whipped cream.

Henri looked up quickly. "Hey, kids. Hope you're hungry."

"Wow, Grandpa," Jade said cautiously. "Thanks for all this."

"Of course. Dig in."

As the twins filled their plates, Henri fidgeted nervously. Finally he said, "Listen, I apologize for yelling yesterday and for being so tense lately. I want you both to feel welcome here and have a good visit. It's no excuse, but . . ." Removing his glasses, he rubbed his eyes. "Things are pretty stressful right now."

Jade reached across the table and squeezed Henri's hand. "It's okay. I'm really sorry."

"Yeah, we're here for you, Grandpa."

The tension drained from the room, and they fell into a comfortable silence. After a few moments, Henri cleared his throat. "I'm blathering on while your breakfast is getting cold. Eat up. I'll meet you downstairs." He stood and left for the museum.

Jade sighed contentedly and took a big bite of her waffle. "Feeling better now?"

Simon chewed thoughtfully on a piece of bacon.

"I guess. I mean, I'm glad he apologized and everything, but he still won't face what's going on with the morgund. He won't even talk about it."

"True," Jade said, her face falling again. "And there's the unplugged security camera and the magic books in his room. Those don't have anything to do with money problems. He's hiding something." She bit her lip. "Feels like we're stuck."

Simon nodded. "Time to ask for help."

After breakfast, the twins spent the morning working in the museum. In what they guessed was an attempt to smooth things over, Henri gave them the afternoon off. Seizing the opportunity, they hurried across the street to the Raven.

Edgar greeted them with a loud caw, while Jacques, who was with a customer, gave them a warm smile. They headed to the Magic and Mythology section and resumed searching books for any reference to the morgund or Catonia.

Soon Jacques came over with Edgar on his shoulder. "How goes the search for your monster?"

Simon closed the book he was holding. "Not great. We wanted to talk to you about that." He paused and looked at Jade, his eyebrows raised. She nodded.

"My curiosity is rising," Jacques said.

Over the next several minutes, the twins told Jacques about Henri's odd behavior and their beliefs about the morgund, finishing by showing him the photo of the empty platform. Edgar was strangely still, seeming to listen as intently as his owner. When they'd finished, Simon asked, "So . . . what do you think?"

Jacques stared off into space for several long moments while gently stroking Edgar's feathers. Finally, he looked at the twins with a solemn expression. "I think perhaps you have been spending too much time in that spooky museum."

Simon's shoulders slumped. "You sound like Grandpa."

"You must understand," Jacques said. "I have lived a long time and have never believed in the supernatural. What you are suggesting is difficult for my old brain to accept."

"But what about the empty platform?" Jade pressed.

Jacques looked troubled. "I confess, I cannot explain that. But I do share your concern about your grandfather. I worry about him lately, especially with Sophie out of town."

"So you'll help us?" Simon asked.

"I will do everything I can to support Henri. As for the morgund, I am afraid that is a step too far for me, at least right now." He gazed at their dejected faces. "I have disappointed you, no? For that, I am sorry. Who knows? Perhaps you will prove me wrong."

The bell above the door jangled, and Jacques walked off.

Simon gazed ruefully at Jade. "I guess we really are on our own."

CHAPTER 23

JADE WOKE the next morning to a pillow hitting her head.

"Hey!" she mumbled groggily. "What was that for?"

"It was love," Simon said.

"I'm touched."

As she stared up at the ceiling, the frustration of their situation came back to her. They'd searched the Raven for hours the previous day and found nothing. Hanging out with Henri last night had been less tense after his apology, but still uncomfortable, as they avoided talking about anything real. They'd all gone to bed early. What could she do to fix this? To make her grandpa understand? A helpless feeling sat on her stomach like a bowling ball.

When the twins came out of their bedroom, Henri wasn't at the table.

"Grandpa must have gotten up early," Simon said as he grabbed a box of cereal.

They ate in sleepy silence before heading down to the museum. Henri wasn't in the gift shop or his office, so the twins wandered into the display rooms. "Grandpa?" Simon called. There was no response.

"Where could he be?" Jade asked.

"Maybe at the Raven?" Simon suggested.

"Jacques never opens this early." Jade tried Henri's cell phone, but a moment later ended the call. "Went right to voicemail. You don't think anything's wrong, do you?"

Heart pounding, Simon pulled out his phone and opened his news app. He sucked in a breath. "There was another attack last night over by the bakery. The victim is in the hospital, but they don't give a name." He looked at Jade, his face ashen. "You don't think . . . ?"

Jade's voice trembled. "Grandpa."

The twins burst out the door and ran down the street. When they finally reached the hospital, they rushed up to the information desk. "Henri . . . Lyon," Simon wheezed, out of breath. "Is he here?"

The young man behind the desk looked up in surprise, then hurriedly typed on his computer. A moment later, he nodded. "Yes, he was admitted to the ER last night and transferred to room 304 this morning."

Jade and Simon raced toward the elevators.

When the elevator doors opened on the third floor, they ran down the hall, scanning room numbers. Finding 304, they hurried inside.

Henri lay in a bed, an oxygen tube in his nose. There were bandages on his face and arms. He looked pale, and his eyes were closed. His silver-rimmed glasses lay on a bedside table.

Jade choked out a sob, and Simon felt like he'd been punched in the gut. How could this be happening? Was he going to live? Gently, he took Henri's hand. "Grandpa?"

Henri didn't stir.

They heard footsteps behind them and turned. A nurse with light brown skin and purple hair entered the room, pausing when she saw the twins. She gave a sympathetic smile. "I'm Danika. Is Henri your grandpa?"

Simon nodded mournfully. "Is he going to be okay?"

Danika stepped forward and put her hands on Simon's shoulders. "Your grandpa is going to be just fine. He's scratched up and took a bite on the arm, but nothing serious."

"So he was attacked?" Jade asked. "Like those other two people?"

Danika hesitated. "His injuries look like they're from an animal attack." She gave a tight smile. "Don't worry. I'm sure the police and animal control will find it soon."

The twins gave each other a knowing look. "Can we stay with him?" Simon asked.

"Of course. We gave him something to help him sleep, but he should be waking up soon." She examined some equipment beside Henri's bed and pressed a few buttons. "I'll be back to check on him in a little while. If you need anything, come find me at the nurses' station."

After she left, Simon turned to Jade. "I think we should call Mom. She deserves to know."

Jade sighed. "I hate interrupting their anniversary trip, but you're right. You can stay here. I'll go in the hall so I don't disturb Grandpa."

Simon stared at Henri, drinking in the familiar lines of his face. He was relieved by the nurse's assurances, but it was still scary seeing his grandpa in a hospital bed, hooked up to strange equipment and looking vulnerable. He thought of the powerful morgund and knew the attack could have been so much worse. Simon's sense of security felt painfully fragile. "Please be okay," he whispered.

A few minutes later, Jade returned.

"What'd you tell her?" Simon asked.

"Just that it was some kind of animal attack, and he'll be fine. She's going to let Grandma know what happened. She was worried about where we'd stay tonight, so I told her he should be released by then. I tried to convince her they didn't need to come back, but she insisted. With the time difference in Greece and having to get a last-minute flight, they won't be here till tomorrow."

Simon nodded grimly. "So that only gives us one more day."

"One more day for what?" Henri croaked.

"Grandpa!" the twins said in unison, pushing closer to the bed.

"How are you feeling?" Jade asked.

Henri tried to smile and winced. "I've been better, but I'll survive. Are you both okay? I've been out of it since I was brought in. Did they call you?"

Jade shook her head. "When we couldn't find you this morning and heard there was another attack, we figured it out."

Henri closed his eyes for a moment with a sigh.

"I'm so sorry to scare you like that. I had my wallet, but I wasn't carrying my phone, so they didn't have my emergency contact numbers. Foolish of me."

"We're just glad you're going to be all right," Simon said.

"What happened?" Jade asked. "We thought you were in your bedroom last night."

Henri gazed at the ceiling. "I was, but I couldn't sleep and decided to go for a walk. That . . . animal . . . came out of nowhere and knocked me down. I don't remember much else."

"What did it look like?" Jade asked.

Henri shifted his eyes to the window. "Not sure. Didn't get a good look."

"Did you hear anything unusual?" Simon asked. "Any strange noises?"

"Noises?" Henri asked. "Like what?"

Simon hesitated, glancing at Jade. If they

mentioned the laughter, they'd have to explain how they'd snuck off to question the first victim. "Um . . . nothing in particular."

"Is this a private party?" said a voice with a French accent.

The twins turned to see Jacques standing in the doorway.

"What are you doing here?" Henri asked in surprise.

"Checking up on my friends, of course."

"But how did you know where we were?" Jade asked.

"When I came down to the Raven this morning, I noticed the door to the museum was standing open. When I found no one inside, I grew concerned. After hearing about the attack last night, I feared the worst and came straight here."

Simon shuffled his feet. "Sorry about leaving the

door open. We were in such a hurry, we must have forgotten to close it."

"I can't blame you for that," Henri said.

"Will you be all right?" Jacques asked.

"Yes, but I'm not sure when I'll get out of here," Henri said. "Can the kids stay with you tonight?"

"Of course."

The twins looked at each other, the same concern mirrored in their eyes. "Um . . . we'll be fine on our own for one night," Jade said. "Mom and Dad will be here tomorrow, and we don't want to bother you, Jacques."

"Nonsense! Edgar will enjoy the extra attention."

Simon blew out a long breath. Finding a way to stop the morgund on their final day had just gotten more complicated.

CHAPTER 24

"I THINK it's that time, you three," Danika said later that morning. "Our patient needs his rest."

The twins and Jacques stood up to leave. Jacques had kept them entertained with stories of the trouble he and Henri had gotten into growing up in their small town in France.

"What should we do about the museum today, Grandpa?" Simon asked.

"Just put a note on the door saying we're closed for the day," Henri said.

Jacques looked grim. "With the way the tourists are staying away from Skull Rock, it will hardly matter."

"No need to talk about that now," Henri said. "Thanks again for taking the kids."

"My pleasure," Jacques said. "They can help me at the shop. We will come back this evening."

They said their goodbyes and made their way downtown. After they put the note on the museum door, Jacques bought them lunch at Café Eiffel.

Edgar greeted them with a loud caw as they entered the Raven. Much to their surprise, the bird flew over and landed on Simon's shoulder.

"Well, well!" Jacques exclaimed. "It appears Edgar has adopted you both into our little family. You should be honored. He is very picky when it comes to people."

"Cool!" Simon said, gently stroking Edgar's feathers with one finger.

"What can we do to help?" Jade asked.

"Collect whatever you need for the night from Henri's apartment," Jacques said. "When you get back, I will show you where you can sleep in my humble abode upstairs." He reached a hand out to Edgar. "Come, bird. They have to go to the museum."

Rather than hop to Jacques's finger, the raven cawed again and turned his back to the man.

"Cheeky creature," Jacques chided. "Apparently, he is quite comfortable on your shoulder."

"Can we take him with us?" Simon asked. "Like you did the other day?"

Jacques shrugged. "Why not? He has adopted you, after all. Be good, Edgar."

The twins walked across the street to the museum, with the raven drawing a few stares. Simon moved with a little swagger, enjoying the attention. Once inside, they headed toward the steps to Henri's apartment. Edgar flew off into the display rooms, cawing loudly.

"Hey!" Simon called. "Come back."

"He'll be fine," Jade said. "Let's go get our stuff. We can bring Grandpa's books from his desk too. Maybe there's something we missed the first time."

Before they reached the stairs, the raven returned, swooping in front of their faces and flapping wildly before landing on a postcard stand. He made a horrible racket.

"What's up with him?" Jade asked. "He's never acted like this before."

Edgar flew back into the museum before turning to caw at them again.

"I think he wants us to follow him," Simon said.

"Anything to shut him up."

When the twins walked into the first display

room, Edgar took off, leading them deeper into the museum. They found him fluttering against the closed doors of the morgund room.

"This is weird," Jade said as she worked her paper clips in the lock.

As she slid the doors aside, Edgar swooped between them and landed on the werehyena's head.

"Whoa," Simon said. "What are the odds of that happening again?"

The raven flew across the room to the red display cabinet full of Sasquatch footprints. He cawed loudly, then returned to the morgund's head. He repeated the pattern, flying back and forth, cawing all the while.

"Is he trying to tell us something?" Jade asked.

"Ravens are supposed to be really smart," Simon said. "But what's he saying?"

"Maybe he wants us to check out that display cabinet."

They moved closer, examining the collection of frighteningly large prints. Edgar, now silent, perched on top of the cabinet and watched them intently.

"See anything unusual?" Simon asked.

"Everything I'm seeing is unusual," Jade replied.

Simon looked closely at the row of prints on the lowest shelf. They sat upright on a blood-red silk cloth. Between them lay a patch of hide covered with long reddish-brown hairs. The display card read *Supposed Yeti Scalp*. The red cloth beneath it was raised slightly.

"Is there something under that?" Simon asked. He opened the glass door of the cabinet and gently lifted the scalp.

"Eww," Jade said. "How can you touch that thing?"

Simon drew back the red silk where the scalp had stood. Hidden beneath the cloth was a black book with a tarnished gold clasp. The worn leather binding was cracked, and the words *Liber de Mortem* were engraved on the cover. Lifting it carefully, he opened the book as Jade crowded close. Poetic-looking entries in a flowing hand filled the pages.

"I think this is Latin," Simon said.

Jade wrinkled her nose. "More creepy drawings. Is it another dark magic book like the ones in Grandpa's room?"

The pages were stiff and yellowed with age. Turning them gently, Simon came upon some sheets of modern white paper stuffed inside. They were covered with handwritten notes in blue ink.

"These are in English," Jade said, scanning the first page. "Maybe they're translations?"

Simon tensed. "There's something about the morgund!" From one of the translated pages, he read, *"If the need arises, use this spell to conjure the morgund. An unholy blend of hyena and human, the beast will awaken at midnight, roaming free until dawn's light draws it back to the place of its creation to rest in a frozen state. The beast will strike terror in the hearts of your enemies, but beware—the will of the morgund is strong. Once created, it is not easily subdued."*

"And there's the conjuring spell! Simon, this is how the morgund was brought to life!"

Trembling, Simon flipped to the next translated page. *"When the morgund is no longer needed, it can be returned to its true state. The reversal spell must be cast while the creature is awake, and can only be performed by an experienced mage with strength of heart."*

"And there's the spell!" Jade cried, reading the translation quickly.

"So we can do it. We can stop the morgund!"

They stared at the book, stunned that they'd actually found what they'd been desperately searching for.

"You'll have to do it," Simon said. "You're the magician."

Jade's eyes bulged. "A pretend one! Card tricks, illusions, rabbit-from-a-hat stuff. This is, like, *sorceress* level. I can't do this!"

"Well, you'd better try, or this thing will keep hurting people."

Jade glanced back at the hulking werehyena, trying to think of another option. With a sinking feeling, she realized there wasn't one. Her expression clouded. "Why would Grandpa hide this book here instead of keeping it with the others?"

"No idea," Simon said. "And I still don't understand his connection to the morgund."

"Me neither. I mean, he just got *attacked*. How could he be involved?"

They were quiet for a moment, lost in a swirl of conflicting thoughts and emotions. Hearts pounding, they gazed at the morgund, its frozen snarl menacing even in the daylight.

Jade swallowed a lump in her throat as she

considered the terrifying reality of the task ahead. Could she really work a spell in the dead of night with a living, breathing monster bearing down on her?

She was about to find out.

CHAPTER 25

"URGH!" JADE growled. "I'm never gonna get this!"

She pushed back from the desk in Jacques's guest room with a sigh and rubbed her temples. *Liber de Mortem* lay in front of her, open to the reversal spell. In the margins around the swirling, hand-written script were drawings of savage werehyenas. A full-color image at the top of the page showed a morgund attacking a village while people fled in terror.

"Are you sure you can't use the English translation?" Simon asked. "It'd be a lot easier to memorize than the Latin."

"I don't think so. History of magic books always say precise wording is really important with spells. I don't think a translation would work."

"Why don't you just write it down so you can read it?"

Jade shook her head and flipped the page. On the ancient parchment were several drawings of complex hand positions. "I have to weave my fingers together in a specific pattern while I recite the spell. I can't do that and hold a piece of paper."

"I could hold it for you."

"But who knows what you'll need to be doing? It's not a short spell. You might have to distract the morgund or something."

"No problem," Simon said, rolling his eyes. "I'll just break into my stand-up routine."

"I know it's a monster, but do we really have to torture the poor thing?" Jade said. "How are you coming with the list of materials for the spell?"

"I'm pretty sure some of the stuff in the museum is pure silver. For the bird feather, I'm hoping Edgar will donate one without pecking our eyes out. I'm not sure how to manage the fire, though. I don't want to burn the museum down."

"What about candles? If they're in holders, that should be pretty safe."

"Nice," Simon said, checking his list. "Okay, that just leaves a mirror. Do you have one?"

"Nope."

"I can try to find one at the drugstore when I go out looking for candles and chalk for the circle. Then I'll search the museum for something silver." Simon headed for the door. "If Jacques asks, tell him I went for ice cream."

"Don't be too long. We're gonna visit Grandpa after dinner."

The rest of the afternoon passed quickly. Jade recited the reversal spell silently to herself while organizing bookshelves in the Raven for Jacques. Simon returned an hour later with a plastic bag in hand.

"What do you have there?" Jacques asked.

"Um . . . just some stuff to give to Grandpa tonight. Candy and a puzzle book."

"That was very thoughtful of you. Why don't you help your sister?"

Simon hurried back to join Jade. "Did you get everything?" she whispered.

He grinned and held up the bag. "Everything but Edgar's feather. I found some silver coins in the museum. Took me a while to figure out where Grandpa kept the keys to that case."

"What are you going to do when you don't have candy and a puzzle book to give to Grandpa tonight? Jacques will notice."

"But I do." He reached in the bag and held up a book and some peanut M&M'S.

Jade raised her eyebrows. "Wow, that was really thoughtful of you, Simon."

"Actually, I got these for me," he said, with a slightly guilty expression. When Jade glared at him, he added, "But I'm going to give them to Grandpa!"

When the Raven closed for the day, they all ate pizza at Jacques's favorite Italian restaurant before spending the evening at the hospital. Henri was much improved and scheduled to be discharged the next morning.

When visiting hours were over, they returned to Jacques's apartment above the Raven. Jade and Simon yawned conspicuously, prompting Jacques to suggest they all head to bed.

The twins waited for Jacques to settle before sneaking down the dark stairwell with their supplies. In the bookshop, they approached Edgar, who stood on his perch near the cash register. The bird looked at them curiously.

"Okay, get the feather," Jade said.

"Me? Why do I have to do it?"

"I learned Latin. And you were in charge of getting the supplies, remember?"

With a sigh, Simon pulled a pair of sunglasses from the bag and slipped them on.

Jade looked at her twin like he'd lost his mind. "What are you doing? It's dark out."

"This is eye protection in case Edgar gets mad." Simon stepped closer to the bird. "Listen, Edgar. We're trying to stop the morgund from hurting people. To do that, I need to pluck one of your feathers. I'm really sorry about this. Please don't kill me."

The raven's eyes widened as he stared at Simon. With a soft caw, he turned his back to them and spread his tail feathers wide. Simon glanced at Jade in surprise, then slowly reached out and grasped Edgar's tail. With his other hand over his face, he gave a quick tug and pulled a feather free.

The raven squawked and beat his wings but didn't attack.

"Thanks, Edgar," Simon said with relief. "This means a lot." He dropped the feather into the bag, and they turned to go.

Before they reached the door, Edgar took flight and landed on Simon's shoulder.

"I think he wants to come with us," Jade said.

"I wouldn't mind the company," Simon said. "Besides, he's a part of this now."

Moments later, two twins and a raven entered a dark museum to take on a monster.

CHAPTER 26

"DOES THIS look right to you?" Simon asked.

Jade studied the chalk circle he'd drawn on the floor around the morgund. Candles, silver coins, a mirror, and Edgar's feather were carefully arranged along its edge. She looked down at the drawing beside the reversal spell in *Liber de Mortem* and swallowed a lump in her throat. "I . . . I think so."

Edgar watched silently from his perch on the Sasquatch prints cabinet. Simon stood and looked at his sister. Her face reflected the same fear that was building inside him like a volcano. "Are you ready with the verbal part?"

Jade nodded, her eyes like twin blue moons. Simon went to the door and, with a deep breath, turned off the overhead light. In the sudden darkness, the flickering candles cast an eerie glow on the morgund, making it appear even more sinister.

The twins walked into the next display room. Once out of sight of the morgund, they dropped down and crawled behind the two-headed taxidermy grizzly that stood nearby. Peering through the bear's legs, they could see one side of the morgund through the doorway. They weren't sure how much awareness the creature had in its frozen state, but since it didn't leave the night of the stakeout, they'd decided to keep out of sight.

An hour crept past. Huddled together in the dark, silent museum, neither twin had trouble staying awake. Their anxiety over what lay ahead left them both on edge. Once the morgund awoke, would the circle hold it long enough for Jade to say the reversal spell? Had they gotten the right items? Did they arrange them correctly? Shivering, Jade placed her head in her hands and tried to slow her galloping heartbeat. Even Simon, lover of all things spooky, shifted uneasily. He remembered all too well the cold terror that had raced through him when he'd seen the morgund in the street.

A low growl disturbed the tomblike silence. The twins stiffened. The morgund's hand slowly drew into a fist, long claws gleaming in the candlelight. The werehyena raised its arms in a long stretch and shook itself before stepping off the platform. It stopped at the edge of the chalk circle. Trembling uncontrollably, Simon and Jade held their breath.

A shriek ripped through the museum, causing the twins to jump. The morgund snarled angrily and paced inside the circle but did not cross it.

"It's working!" Simon said. "Let's go!"

Jumping to their feet, the twins rushed into the room. The morgund turned toward them with a spine-tingling roar, its face contorted in fury.

"Do it!" Simon yelled.

Quivering from head to toe, Jade wove her fingers together as the book directed and began reciting the spell, stumbling over the Latin in her fright. The morgund roared again, slashing the air with its razor-sharp claws in the direction of the twins.

Jade started again, steadier this time as she saw the monster appeared to be trapped in the magic circle. The morgund began to twitch as the spell rolled over it, spinning around and stalking wildly within its invisible cage.

"You're doing it!" Simon cried.

Jade stepped forward, reciting the words with more power. She took a shuddering breath as she neared the end of the spell. It was almost over.

The morgund leaped, not toward them but straight up like a rocket. It caught a ceiling beam overhead, sinking its claws into the thick wood. Swinging its legs up, the beast latched on with its toe claws.

Then it began to crawl along the beam toward the twins.

Jade faltered, the words of the spell dying on her lips.

Appearing to strain with effort, the morgund pulled itself along, its thigh muscles and biceps bulging. Moments later, it released its grip on the beam and, twisting in midair, landed with catlike grace on the museum floor.

Outside the circle.

The blood drained from Jade's face as Simon whimpered and stood quaking with terror. The monster stepped toward them.

"Run!" Simon yelled.

They turned and raced for the exit, but the morgund was faster. Reaching the door, the beast spun and crouched low, barring their escape. Jade and Simon slid to a stop and backed away.

"Start again!" Simon urged.

Trembling violently, Jade tore her gaze from the morgund's face, breaking the paralyzing horror of its red-eyed glare. "What are *you* gonna do?"

"Buy you some time." Picking up a glass skull, Simon threw it at the morgund's head. The beast slapped it from the air with a huge hand. The skull shattered against the gargoyle-shaped footstool, sending shards of glass flying like shrapnel.

Jade began the spell again while maneuvering through the displays, trying to get as far from the monster as possible. Simon searched wildly for something he could use to defend himself. His retreating foot kicked the mirror lying on the chalk circle. Snatching it up, he held it out like a tiny shield as the morgund raced toward him.

Skidding on the wood floor, the beast stopped and gazed into the mirror. With a wail, it threw up its arms and stumbled backward. Simon stared at the mirror in wonder. In a burst of inspiration, he moved toward the morgund, thrusting the mirror in its face. The beast howled again and retreated. Simon pressed his advantage until the morgund's back was against the wall. With a shout of triumph, he stepped closer.

Too close. The morgund's claws shot out and raked across Simon's wrist. He cried out in pain as the mirror flew through the air and smashed on the floor.

Cradling his wounded arm, Simon backpedaled. "Jade, hurry!"

Distracted by Simon's injury, Jade paused her

recitation. *Wait. What was the next line?* She couldn't remember. "I lost it!" she wailed.

"Then find it!" Simon yelled. In desperation, he grabbed one of the silver coins from the floor and threw it at the charging morgund. The coin simply bounced off the monster's chest, but he was rewarded with a sharp yelp. Without slowing, the morgund plowed into Simon, driving him to the floor. It hovered over him, jaws wide. A thick band of saliva dripped onto Simon's cheek.

His eyes wide with terror, Simon reached out frantically, trying to find some kind of weapon. His hand closed on another silver coin arranged on the circle. Instinctively, he pressed it against the morgund's shoulder. There was a sizzling sound, and the beast howled in pain before staggering back, clutching the spot the coin had touched. The stench of burnt hair filled in the room.

While Jade desperately restarted the spell, Simon scrambled to his feet, accidentally knocking over one of the candles. The heavy glass holder rolled across the wooden floor and came to rest against a tapestry hanging near Jade. The bottom fringe dangled into the still-flickering candle. The fabric caught, and soon flames licked eagerly over the dry material.

"Fire!" cried Simon, looking around wildly for an extinguisher.

Now wary of Simon, the morgund closed in on Jade. As she watched the approaching beast, her mind went horrifyingly blank. The spell was gone.

The flames burned through the cloth ties connecting the tapestry to the wall, and it crashed to the floor in a shower of sparks. The morgund reached the display case where Jade crouched, looming over her with a wicked grin. She gazed into the beast's eyes and froze in terror like a bird before a cobra.

Then Jade thought of her grandparents. Her mom and dad. Simon. What would losing her do to them? She couldn't let that happen. She had to fight.

Grabbing an unburnt edge of the fallen tapestry, Jade leaped up with a wild yell and threw the burning fabric over the morgund. Shrieking in fright and pain, the creature stumbled back, clawing at its flaming shroud.

"Come on!" Simon shouted.

She raced to her brother, but the maddened creature stood between them and the exit. Before they could maneuver around it, the morgund flung off the burning tapestry. It landed in the pool at the base of the simulated waterfall. A hiss of steam rose up as the water doused the flames. Chest heaving, fur smoking, the beast pierced the twins with a glare so full of malice that it stole their breath. Huddled together, they pressed their backs against the wall, looking desperately for a place to run.

The morgund stalked forward, herding the twins into a corner until it towered over them, claws spread wide, jaws gaping. As Jade looked helplessly into the creature's face, she remembered with horror why the werehyena was so feared—it ate children.

At that moment, the morgund began to laugh. It was the most terrifying sound the twins had ever heard. The twisted laughter echoed through the room, mocking their impending doom.

Simon reached out again with the silver coin, but the morgund was ready. It caught his wrist in one huge hand and squeezed. Simon dropped the coin with a cry, and it rolled away. Jade jumped forward with a scream of horror-filled rage and beat the morgund's chest with her bare fists. It shrugged off the attack and threw her to the ground, pinning her with a huge foot.

With a peal of crazed laughter, the beast raised its clawed hand to deliver the final blow.

CHAPTER 27

CAWING WILDLY, Edgar flew into the morgund's face, scratching with his talons. The raven stabbed relentlessly with his beak at the werehyena's eyes. The morgund released Simon and retreated, swatting at the darting bird, eyes clenched protectively.

Simon pulled his sister to her feet. "Come on, Jade. We need you!"

"I . . . I can't do it!" she wailed, her tear-streaked face stained with smoke.

"Yes, you *can*. The book said the spell needs to be performed by an experienced magician. That's you! You can do this!"

Jade desperately tried to ignore the howls of the morgund, kept at bay for the moment by the swooping Edgar. She began again, haltingly at first, then stronger. Jade's pace increased, her confidence growing as the words came back to her with startling clarity.

As she neared the end of the spell, the morgund's flailing hand finally connected with the darting raven. Edgar gave a heartrending screech before hitting the wall with a muffled crunch. His limp form fell to the floor and lay still. Roaring in triumph, the morgund strode toward the twins.

"Edgar!" Simon cried in dismay, taking a step toward the fallen bird. Then he caught himself and turned back to Jade. "Don't stop! Finish it!"

She continued the spell, the words spilling out

faster and faster. As the morgund loomed above them, Jade, her voice rising to a crescendo, uttered the final phrase.

The morgund froze. The twins looked up at the monster, mouths open, eyes wide. Its head shook. Then its arms spasmed. It spun around, staggering as its whole body convulsed. Falling to the floor, the morgund writhed wildly, shrieking horribly. It began to shrink, its form shifting, limbs contracting, face contorting.

Moments later, it was over.

Jade and Simon stared at the still form lying on the floor before them and gasped.

It was Grandma Sophie.

CHAPTER 28

FROZEN WITH shock, the twins gazed at Sophie in disbelief.

She groaned.

"Grandma!" Jade cried, rushing forward. Taking a purple cape from a suit of armor, she draped it over her grandmother.

"Where . . . where am I?" Sophie asked, pushing herself into a sitting position. "What happened? Jade, Simon, is that you?"

"We're here," Jade said as she threw her arms around Sophie. "But you . . . how?"

"Oh, child," Sophie said, her memory flooding back as she glanced around the room. She closed her eyes, and a look of deep sorrow swept over her face. "I'm back now, fool that I am."

Jade pulled away and touched Sophie's cheek as if to make sure she was real.

Simon knelt beside them, gazing at his grandmother in awe. "You? *You* were the morgund? But . . . how? I thought you were in France!"

"France?" Sophie groaned bitterly. "Oh, what have I put you all through? Can you ever forgive me? I'm not sure I'll be able to forgive myself."

"Of course!" Jade cried. "But forgive you for what?"

"For being an overly curious, stubborn old woman." She sighed deeply. "Henri and I bought a library collection at an estate auction that included old magic books. I was delighted, but some of them focused on dark magic. One in particular wasn't a history book—it was practical. Henri saw the danger and insisted we get rid of it immediately. I agreed." She shook her head slowly in regret. "But curiosity and pride got the best of me. I studied the book in secret, thinking I could handle it. After I gathered the supplies and recited the morgund incantation, a strange feeling crept over me, so I hid the book in a cabinet and went to lie down. My skin began to prickle, and golden hairs started growing on my arm. Then I realized what I'd done." She gazed at the twins with a mournful expression. "That's the last thing I remember."

"Whoa," Simon said, his brain racing to process his grandma's story. "You turned *yourself* into the morgund?"

Sophie nodded miserably. "Apparently so. I never

thought those spells would actually work. But how did you free me?"

"We've been searching for a way to stop the attacks," Jade said. "We finally found the book and performed the reversal spell. But we never dreamed it was you!"

"Attacks?" Sophie said in alarm. "What do you mean?"

As the twins shared a meaningful look, Edgar fluttered fitfully on the floor. Shaking off the blow, he flew to the top of the Sasquatch cabinet and watched the reunion quietly. With sighs of relief, Jade and Simon gazed gratefully at the raven before turning back to Sophie, who'd been too distracted to notice Edgar.

"So you have no memory of your time as the morgund?" Simon asked slowly.

Sophie's forehead furrowed. "None. I don't remember anything."

"Well," Jade said, shifting uncomfortably. "You . . . I mean, the morgund . . . came to life at night. You left the museum and ran around town, breaking into businesses and . . ." She paused awkwardly.

"And what?" Sophie pressed. "What did I do?"

Simon sighed. "You attacked some people. Put them in the hospital."

Sophie gasped, her hands coming to her mouth. "No! Oh, what have I done?" she whispered miserably. Then her eyes snapped up, staring hard at the twins. "Where is Henri?"

💀

CHAPTER 29

SOPHIE AND the twins hurried through the quiet hospital lobby. As it was well after visiting hours, they climbed a back stairwell to avoid the night staff and made it to Henri's room without being stopped. They rushed inside and found him asleep, a bedside light casting a dim glow over his bandaged face.

Sophie gave a small cry and grasped Henri's hand as tears streamed down her cheeks. His eyelids fluttered open, and his gaze fell on his wife. For a moment he simply stared before recognition flooded his eyes. "Am I dreaming? Sophie, is that really you?"

She nodded, too overcome to speak, and placed her hand gently on his face. Then they were in each other's arms, crying, laughing, and murmuring in French. Simon and Jade looked on, faces beaming and eyes full of tears.

When Sophie finally stepped back, Henri's expression grew pained. "I'm so sorry. I tried everything, but I couldn't find a way to help. I failed you."

She gazed at him in disbelief. "Failed me? *I'm* the one who's sorry. You warned me about that blasted book, and I let my stubborn pride and curiosity get the best of me. What agony I must have put you through. Can you ever forgive me?"

Henri chuckled softly. "I knew what I was getting into when we married. You take me on wild rides, but you're worth every second. You're for-given. I wouldn't trade you for the world."

Sophie raised Henri's hand and kissed it.

"So you *knew* Grandma was the morgund?" Simon asked Henri, his eyes wide.

Henri nodded ruefully. "I'm so sorry I lied to you. When I discovered Sophie missing and the morgund in the museum, I realized what must have happened. But however hard I searched, I couldn't find that awful book. I studied the other magic volumes from the collection, tried saying differ-ent spells over her, even asked Jacques for books on dark magic. Nothing helped." His eyes closed briefly at the painful memory. "No one would have believed the truth, so I pretended Sophie had gone on a trip. I didn't know what else to do." Turning to Sophie, he asked, "How in the world did you get free?"

She nodded toward Jade and Simon. "We have brilliant grandchildren."

Simon grinned and tightened the dustcloth he'd wrapped around the cuts on his arm. "I should probably be humble, but you're right, we are kind of awesome. We figured out there was a connection between the morgund and everything going on in town. When you acted weird about it, we kept investigating and found the magic books in your desk and the unplugged security camera. We knew you were involved, but didn't know how."

"We thought that if the morgund was created by magic, maybe it could be stopped the same way," Jade said. "Edgar helped us find the book hidden in the museum, and we used it to perform the reversal spell."

"Edgar?" Henri said in surprise. "Jacques's *raven* led you to the book?"

"And he helped us fight off . . ." Simon paused

awkwardly and glanced at Sophie. "Well . . . Grandma."

For the first time since the twins arrived that summer, Henri actually laughed. "I guess I've accepted stranger things lately." He looked adoringly at Sophie and wiped his eyes before turning back to the twins. "I tried to talk your mom out of bringing you here, but she's as stubborn as I am. So I protected you kids the best I could with the security door while continuing to search for a way to free Sophie. I tried locking her in, and even put bars on the window, but the morgund was too strong and clever. When the attacks started, I knew I had to do something, so I went out at night, hoping to stop her. That's what I was doing when . . . well, when I ended up here."

Henri and Sophie shared a sad smile. They all grew quiet, each processing the moment in their own way.

Finally, Jade asked, "Grandpa, should you call Jacques? I don't want him to worry if he finds us missing. And you should probably mention we left Edgar at the museum."

Henri dialed Jacques, putting the phone on speaker. A few moments later, a sleepy voice answered.

"Henri, is that you? Are you all right?"

"I'm fine, Jacques. Sorry to wake you, but I wanted you to know the kids are with me." He looked at his wife and grinned. "Sophie came home unexpectedly."

CHAPTER 30

"DAD!" ISABELLE cried as she rushed across Henri's living room to hug her father. "You should be sitting down. Are you all right?"

"I'm fine, honey," Henri said. "The hospital released me this morning. You both must be exhausted after your flight." He nodded to his son-in-law. "Hey, Jack. Sorry I ruined your anniversary trip."

"Don't be ridiculous, Henri," Jack said. "We're just glad you're okay."

"So what happened?" Isabelle asked. "Have they caught the animal that attacked you? Was it a bear?"

Henri darted a glance at the twins. "Not yet. But there haven't been any sightings since the attack, so it probably moved on. I don't think we have to worry about it anymore."

Jade remained silent. Simon, knowing he had a lousy poker face, stared at his shoes. The twins and their grandparents had decided to keep the real story a secret. Isabelle and Jack probably wouldn't have believed them anyway.

"That bear took one bite of Henri and gave up its taste for humans," Sophie said as she stepped from the bedroom.

"Mom!" Isabelle exclaimed. "I didn't know you were back already. You never answered my calls about Dad."

"Sorry, honey. That must have been during my flight home."

"How's Aunt Geneviève?"

Sophie hesitated, then said with a smile, "Everything's fine now, honey. Just fine."

CHAPTER 31

Five days later . . .

"IS THAT the last bag?" Jack asked before closing the car's trunk.

The whole family gathered in front of the museum. The boardwalk was crowded with tourists again, and the museum was doing a brisk business. Jade sniffed and tucked her hair behind her ears as it fluttered in the ocean breeze. "I'm going to miss you both so much," she said as she hugged her grandparents.

"We'll miss you all, too," Sophie said.

"I can't wait until we come next summer," Simon said. "I've got some ideas for new displays."

Henri chuckled. "I look forward to hearing them. Who knows, maybe you'll run this place someday."

Sophie said with a wink, "Hopefully things will be much calmer on your next visit."

"All right, you two," Isabelle said to the twins. "Time to load up." After she hugged her parents, they piled into the car and drove off down Ocean-side Lane as Henri and Sophie waved.

When the car was out of sight, Sophie sighed contentedly. "Come on, I'll make lunch. I'm so glad things are finally back to normal."

"Me too, my love," Henri replied. "Me too."

As they turned to head into the museum, Henri scratched distractedly at his forearm where his bite wound was healing. Nestled within the ring of scars, a small patch of golden fur was beginning to grow.

ACKNOWLEDGMENTS

ALTHOUGH THIS is my fourth published book, it's the first time I'm writing an acknowledgment with books on the shelf. While I would be remiss not to thank my awesome family, Lisa, Kilian, and Kennedy; my stalwart agent, Michael Bourret; and my incredible team at Penguin Young Readers, I want to focus my gratitude this time around on some standout people who helped the Monsterious series burst into the world.

To Matt Phipps for taking the editorial reins on this book with your customary class, grace, energy, and insight. I'm incredibly lucky to partner with you on this journey!

To Jordana Kulak for your endless enthusiasm, creativity, support, and professionalism. You are a dream publicist!

To Nicole Caliro for your excellent help in organizing my first book tour. I'll always be grateful!

To Stacey Byl, friend and teacher extraordinaire, for saving the Michigan leg of my tour. You know what I mean.

To all the librarians and teachers who welcomed me into your schools to talk with your students. I am incredibly grateful to you for giving a debut author like me a great start.

To Kim Derting and the whole Cavalcade of Authors West team for inviting me to my first author festival.

To podcasters Marissa Meyer at *The Happy Writer*, Melissa Thom at *Joyful Learning*, Beth McMullen and Lisa Schmid at *Writers with Wrinkles*, and Ari at *Strawberry Milkshake* for having me on their shows. To writing coach Kate Penndorf at Much Ado About Writing and Sophie Nogar at Second Star to the Right Books for their video interviews. To *Spooky Middle Grade*, *Feed Your Fiction Addiction*, *Literary Rambles*, *YA Book Nerd*, and *From the Mixed-Up Files* for your blog interviews. I am forever grateful to you for spreading the word about Monsterious!

To all the bookstores who hosted my events and are carrying my books. I'm so humbled and grateful! A special shout-out for above-and-beyond support from Changing Hands Bookstore (Tempe, AZ), The Wandering Jellyfish (Niwot, CO), Children's Book World

(Los Angeles, CA), Capital Books on K (Sacramento, CA), Second Star to the Right Books (Denver, CO), Warwick's (La Jolla, CA), Turning the Page (Monroe, CT), RJ Julia Booksellers (Madison, CT), and the Barnes & Noble Booksellers in Holland, MI; Grandville, MI; Muskegon, MI; Gilbert, AZ; and Chandler, AZ. You are all rock stars!

Finally, to all the passionate readers who have listened to my talks, come to my events, bought my books, shared on social media, and encouraged me through the launch of Monsterious. I could not do this without you, and I wouldn't want to try. Thank you for your incredible support. Here's to more spooky adventures!

Photo © Kennedy McMann

As a professional musician, **Matt McMann** played an NFL stadium, a cruise ship, and the International Twins Convention. Now he writes the kind of spooky mystery-adventure books he loved as a kid. He's hiked the Pacific Northwest, cruised Loch Ness, and chased a ghost on a mountain. While he missed Bigfoot and Nessie, he caught the ghost. He enjoys brainstorming new books with his wife, *New York Times* bestselling author Lisa McMann; viewing his son Kilian McMann's artwork; and watching his daughter, actor Kennedy McMann, on television.

You can visit Matt at
MattMcMann.com

And follow him on Instagram and Twitter
@Matt_McMann

LOOK OUT FOR MORE THRILLS AND CHILLS IN THE MONSTERIOUS SERIES!

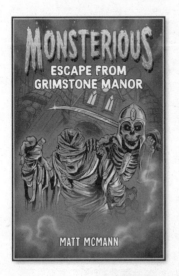

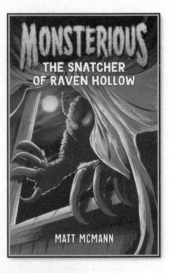

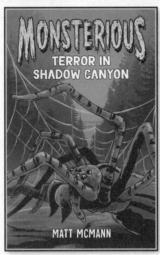